My
Life
as a
girl

My
Life

as a

girl

BY ELIZABETH MOSIER

Random House New York

www.randomhouse.com/kids

Library of Congress Cataloging-in-Publication Data
Mosier, Elizabeth.
My life as a girl / by Elizabeth Mosier. p. cm. SUMMARY: During her
last summer in Phoenix, Arizona, before going to an eastern college,
eighteen-year-old Jaime works two waitress jobs and plans her escape
from a life forever changed by her father's felony trial.
ISBN 0-679-89035-1 (trade). — ISBN 0-679-99035-6 (lib. bdg.)
[1. College—Fiction. 2. Waiters and waitresses—Fiction.
3. Phoenix (Ariz.)—Fiction.] I. Title. PZ7.M8487My 1999
Fiction—dc21 98-8688

Printed in the United States of America
10 9 8 7 6 5 4 3 2 1

For my girls

chapter

one

The day Buddy crashed the campus, Bryn Mawr was in hibernation, suspended in an eerie calm called "reading period" before a week of winter exams. Without the structure of classes, students were stunned; we slept in for the first time all semester, slid into the day sipping coffee and reading the paper, sat mesmerized at our computers answering e-mail. That this brain freeze went on amid white-blanketed fields and trees with crystal sleeves seems incredible, too perfect, even, for a letter to my mom, but that's the way it was. We waited, in those first dark days of December, for the blue books to be offered, for the chance to sharpen our pencils and prove ourselves. There was an optimistic chill in the air, an echo of industry in the tense flapping of the college flag atop the old library, a gray stone castle called Thomas Hall. It made a very pretty picture, but all was not exactly well.

Elaine Simon lounged in the living room as she had all semester, avoiding writing an English paper that had been extended into eternity by her indulgent dean. That morning, I'd asked to borrow her Hi-Liter,

My
Life

as a

girl

and had been panic-stricken by the state of her room. Dirty clothes tumbled off the bed and out of baskets, while her closet stood empty. There were books and candy wrappers everywhere, a dead fern fossilized on the dresser top. This was my idea of hell, a landing place for failure. How could a person live this way? Why would Elaine—smarter than smart, rumored to be summa cum laude—sabotage herself?

"It's in the top desk drawer," Elaine called out from the living room as I hesitated in her doorway. "Left side, next to the box of paper clips." I stepped over the title page of her English thesis, marked with a 4.0 and a boot-shaped sample of mud, and pulled open the drawer. There, her school supplies were alphabetized and labeled, stored in bright-colored compartments. I shuddered; her secret neatness alarmed me more than her public disarray. Quickly, I grabbed the Hi-Liter and closed the drawer.

That Elaine was a senior made the discovery all the more troubling. The seniors were harbingers of our own futures, and so we first-years watched them the way we watched our mothers, with a keen eye and all-too-easy criticism that increased in intensity as exams approached. There they were in the computer center, begging the student supervisor to keep the printers on for just five more minutes so they could print out another near-perfect draft. There they were floating down the hall in a yeasty-brew cloud after an evening at Creepers, where they'd tried to talk art history with

some guy from Villanova who would have preferred to converse with his hands. There they
were in suits and heels in the dining halls, on
their way to or from job interviews. Nothing like
a crisply pressed suit among the jeans and
sweatshirts to turn table conversation from the
life of the mind to the dreaded life that was "after."

There hadn't been a decent campus party since
Thanksgiving, and we naturally blamed the seniors for
this sorry lack of social life. We were primed for any
kind of excitement, any cure for the communicable
disease of no play, all work. And so it was a weird
relief, almost a celebration, when Buddy arrived at
Merion Hall on that exquisite winter morning, hellbent
on bringing me home.

I saw the Mustang through the living room window as I
curled up on the window seat next to my roommate
Amanda, reading Virginia Woolf's *A Room of One's
Own.* I was writing a paper on the concept of psycho-
logical space, and though I'd discussed the book with
conviction in English class, I had never actually finished it. Idly, with my index finger inserted between
pages as a bookmark, I watched the car slow down and
park crookedly on the road alongside the dorm. I noted
that it was a Mustang, but its blood-colored paint job
(Buddy's was white) muffled what might have otherwise been a rousing alarm.

In Taylor Tower, the bell began to ring eleven, a
reminder that time hadn't stilled after all. It was a

My
Life
as a

girl

senior privilege to ring the bell when you'd finished your spring finals, and I was already
looking forward to my chance to pull the rope.
Who would I be then? I listened to the chime
peal and fade repeatedly. Listening, I became
aware of myself looking out the window, then
aware of my awareness, until I was watching myself
from outside my body, at a six-foot remove.

From that perspective, my life appeared simple
and mechanical—a stack of boxes within boxes—and
my sole purpose that of opening them, revealing myself
to myself. I thought I understood Woolf perfectly as I
came back into my body by slow degrees: college was
a four-year residency in a room of one's own. For me,
Bryn Mawr was a place where my past couldn't reach
me, a place where I could reinvent myself.

That is, until my past pushed open the door of the
wrongly red Mustang and staggered out onto the icy
road.

He was wild-haired and wide-eyed, looking as
though he'd driven the 3,000 miles from Phoenix
straight through, in under eight hours. "Oh, God," I
said, dropping my book to the floor.

Amanda looked up. "What, is He here?"

"It's Buddy," I said, yanking the curtains closed.

Amanda nudged me aside and yanked the curtains
open again. "Buddy?" she said.

Buddy. He leaned against his car door, rubbing his
palms on his jeans as he looked around. He was hat-
less, maybe as camouflage, but his boots and bare

hands screamed Arizona louder than his license plates did. My friend Rosa had seen him during Thanksgiving break, and he'd said then that he would find me. But the threat had seemed ridiculous, B-movie dialogue, much like Buddy's exaggerated claim to eternal love. And yet here he was. At my college. Taking in the gray, Gothic architecture with what, I couldn't help feeling, was an inadequate amount of awe.

"He's shorter than I pictured," said Amanda.

"Wow," said Elaine, peering over our shoulders. "What the hell is that?"

"It's Jaime's boyfriend."

"Here for the weekend?"

"He's not my boyfriend!" I said.

"Summer romance," Amanda clarified.

I whispered, "How did he know I was *here?*"

"I thought he had a white car," said Amanda.

"He does—he *did.*" Looking more closely at the Mustang, I saw—or imagined—cool streaks of white paint showing through the red.

The three of us sucked in our breath as Buddy began to unbutton his jeans. I winced, and glanced up to the second floor of Taylor, sure I'd find my dean framed there in one of the windows, her proud posture invoking Bryn Mawr's history of women's achievement as she observed this rude, blue-jeaned boy getting ready to piss in the street. Instead, Buddy retucked his rodeo shirt and rebuttoned, then licked his palm and ran it over his hair. He stooped to check himself out in the side mirror, and with that last hopeful gesture, he almost had me again. I gripped the edge of the window seat as he turned and began to walk toward Merion.

"Apparently, the boy did his homework," said Elaine. "He seems to know exactly where he's going."

I headed for the staircase, saying, "That would be a first."

I planned to take the stairs three at a time to the attic, where I could hide behind the old lamps and steamer trunks for the rest of my life. I got as far as the first step, then stood there motionless, clutching the carved wood owl that decorated the banister.

"Do you think he just wants to talk?" Amanda asked me as Buddy began first to knock and then, seconds later, to pound.

"I don't know what he wants," I said, though I guessed the possibilities included reunion or revenge.

"Should I call Security?" asked Elaine, her eyes shining. How typical for Elaine to view Buddy as an excuse to procrastinate.

"Oh, Elaine, don't overreact!" I said, rolling my eyes at Amanda. I'd explained away my thing with Buddy as curiosity, an adventure, even as an act of charity. But the truth was, my continuing desire for him, despite everything, bewildered and depressed me.

"He's not going to hurt you, Jaime, is he?" asked Amanda.

"Of course not," I said.

"Well," Elaine said smugly, "someone should definitely call the fashion police." She patted my cheek as a mother would, as if to remind me that better taste in boyfriends came with seniority.

"He's obviously upset," said Amanda. "Are you going to let him in?"

"I don't know," I said. So far, my life here/my life there had run nicely parallel on tracks separated by 3,000 miles. Now my secret life was about to force its way into my dormitory and spill its mess all over the floor.

As Buddy pounded harder, room doors began opening up and down the hall.

"Someone get that, will you?" yelled Lila-from-Louisiana, much admired for her shopping-mall glamour. She leaned against her door in an emerald satin robe.

"It's Jaime's boyfriend," said Melissa, a sophomore from the Midwest, who was obsessed with enforcing the honor code.

"He's not my boyfriend," I said.

"Maybe not," said Melissa, her expression one of cemented pleasance. "But he's your responsibility."

"What's the problem?" asked Lila, arranging herself on the piano bench, her arms folded across her chest. "Let the guy in. This isn't the fifties, you know, with that old one-foot-on-the-floor rule."

Melissa's smile was still pasted in place. "May I

remind you, Lila," she said, "that privacy is one of the rights one can reasonably expect when one chooses a single-sex dorm?"

"Jaime!" Buddy bellowed. I hopped back a half step and fell on my butt on the stair. "Open up! It's Buddy!"

"Security's coming!" yelled Elaine from her doorway.

"Elaine, you didn't need to do that," Amanda snapped. "Did she, Jaime?"

"No," I said, less certain now.

A group of onlookers had gathered in the living room, where once upon a time, proper young ladies would arrange to meet their dates. They formed a Red Rover line across the entry, all eyes trained on the door.

Time stopped—as it sometimes did in writing conferences with my English professor, who was always on me to "support my ideas with evidence from the text." Those meetings were excruciating; I would agree to rewrite the whole paper just to get out of her office, to spare myself from looking too closely at my mistakes.

Now, as Buddy demanded to be let in, I felt the same cold fear I did at the end of one of those conferences, when what I'd thought was a well-built argument had completely fallen apart. The only way out of that feeling was to crumple up the paper and start over. Or, in this case, to tell the truth about Buddy—and about who Jaime Cody really was.

That was the beginning, as blind and misguided as most beginnings are. I glanced back once more at my hallmates, then walked to the front door and unlatched the lock.

My
Life
as a
girl

chapter

two

"It's freezing out there," Buddy said, pushing past me as I took a quick inventory of his pants, his hands, his pockets, hoping not to discover the glint or poke of a gun. "You like living here, Jaime? At the North Pole?" Dirty slush fell from his snakeskin boots as he stood in place and stomped the Persian rug.

I opened my mouth to speak of the virtues of pure wool versus polyester, the strategy of layering, the heat conservation provided by a hat. I'd learned to dress for the weather; Amanda had even loaned me her Pendleton scarf. But Buddy wasn't waiting for an answer. He was scanning the room, grinning at my hallmates as though he'd said something smart.

"How's it going," Buddy said, his gaze lingering a beat too long on Lila, who sat up straight and clutched her robe closed. His eyes looked more cunning than I remembered, darting and rolling in their bloodshot rims. His hair, tangled and surf-blond in the summer, was now flat and streaked with channel-surfer brown. His nose, fringed by a junior mustache, looked some-what rubbery against the yellow tone of his faded tan.

And yet he strutted around the foyer in his black suede buffalo jacket as if he'd invented sexy. In a way, for me, he had.

"I'm Buddy," he said.

"Yes," said Melissa, with perfect disdain. "We heard."

"Sorry about all the noise," he said. "I just needed to talk to my girlfriend, is all."

Amanda raised her eyebrows. I shook my head at her: *Don't ask.*

A few of the women smiled back at Buddy. I knew they were mentally making him over: dressing him in plaid flannel, placing a guitar or a book of poems in his hand. We all watched as Buddy shrugged out of his coat and tossed it onto the back of a chair. I felt a twinge of possessiveness when he leaned, rebel-like, against the antique iron radiator.

"Damn!" Buddy said, leaping forward as the steam heat branded his butt. I looked away, disowning him. "Damn!" he said again.

"What are you doing here?" I blurted. "Did you dig your way out of the Maricopa County jail?"

"That was bogus," he said. "There wasn't any proof."

"Then you got off on a technicality," I told him. "You just walked away from what you did."

"You're one to be talking," said Buddy. "You thought you could just leave, join some convent, and not even bother to tell me?"

"It's not a convent," I said. "It's called college."

My
Life

as a

girl

Lila said, "There are plenty of men at Haverford."

"Well, it's clear we've reached an impasse," said Melissa, with measured, Midwestern calm.

Buddy snapped his head in their direction, so fast I heard his neck crack. "What was that?" he said.

"Impasse, an obstacle," said Melissa. "I'd recommend mediation."

"Not you," said Buddy. "Her." He turned to Lila, and asked, "Did you just say *men?*"

"There's one in my French class," volunteered Amy, a cheerful sophomore from Connecticut who led Admissions tours.

Buddy sneered. "Now I get it."

"You don't get anything," I said, brushing past him.

"You go, girl!" someone said.

"Jaime, don't leave!" Buddy cried, grabbing for my arm.

I turned around when he caught me, and saw a makeshift bandage peeking out from under his shirt cuff. His wrist was wrapped with gauze, bled through with rusty red. Buddy looked at me defiantly. Behind me, someone gasped; someone else whispered "suicide."

It was just more of Buddy's conniving; the stain was iodine. Still, I took his arm and turned it tenderly, pretending to inspect the bandage. "What happened here?" I asked. As I did this, I was aware of a story unfolding, a story that could explain Buddy and my crazy connection to him.

"What do you think happened?" Buddy said. He was ready to concede the trick, but I wasn't going to let him off so easily. A part of me wished that he really had hurt himself.

"Why did you do it?" I coached him. The room was quiet, so quiet I heard Amanda (a closet romance reader) take in her breath. I knew what she was thinking, could almost picture the neon pink cover showing Buddy and me embracing, the overblown title in italics: *My Love Saved His Life*.

But Buddy was no hero, and this scene was from a disaster movie, not a romance. "Why not?" Buddy said finally, pulling his arm away roughly and tugging his cuff back over his pseudo-wound. He pondered for a moment, as if searching for just the right words. Finally, the effort was too much for him. "You wouldn't believe me, anyway," he said, and took aim at the wall.

"Buddy!" I yelled as he stomped out of Merion to pack his fist with a handful of snow. I ran after him. "Come here," I said, and he obeyed like a forlorn dog. I quickly unwrapped his wrist and tied the gauze around his scraped knuckles. When I'd finished, he said, "That was just a joke," nodding at the rusty-looking ribbon.

"Well, it bombed," I said. "You stay here. I'm getting your coat."

In the living room, the gray-haired cop we called Security stood in the center of a circle of curious

My
Life

as a

girl

women, holding Buddy's buffalo jacket at arm's length. "This your boyfriend's?" he asked me when I entered.

"He's not my boyfriend," I insisted.

"Whoever he is," said Security, "these girls say he's disturbing the peace."

"He's leaving now," I said. "I'm just coming to get his coat."

"Allow me," said Security, like some sort of dorm dad. "I'd like to speak to this, this Bobby."

"Buddy," I said. I handed over the jacket and followed him out.

Among his long list of offenses, Buddy had presumed to park in a space reserved for professors, and so he'd been ordered, first, to move his car. Park as far from Merion Hall as possible, Security had advised him. Preferably in Arizona.

I watched from the front steps as Buddy trudged back out to the Mustang, cursing under his breath so steadily he left a vapor trail. He opened the passenger door first and scooted over to the driver's seat. Then he sat there, engine running, waiting for me.

"Come on, now," said Security, guiding my shoulder in the direction of the dorm.

"I need to say good-bye first," I said, trying to shrug off his hand without seeming impolite. "I mean, he came all this way."

"Crazy, if you ask me," said Security.

"He's not crazy, he's just..."

"In love?" he said. He assumed a speech-making posture, leaning into the porch rail. "That's not love," he said dismissively. "I'll tell you, dear, in my day…"

Listening to him ramble on, I had a revelation: I didn't need permission. Even after a semester in college, clear across the country from my parents, this fact was still, sometimes, news to me. I could do what I wanted. If only I could figure out what I wanted to do.

The door swung open behind us. "I'm going to the library," Amanda said as she helped me into the coat she'd brought down for me. She bent near my ear and whispered, "In case you need the room."

"Thanks," I said uncertainly. "But I don't think—"

"Tell me later," Amanda said as she hurried down the steps. She called back over her shoulder, "And don't leave anything out."

And then, miraculously, people went back to what they'd been doing, as if Buddy were a cowboy clown at the rodeo, sideshow to the drama in the center ring. Melissa slung her backpack over her shoulder and followed Amanda to the library. Lila, now dressed, was on her way to the café to fill her empty mug. Elaine moved with unusual speed in the direction of the computer center. Security checked the lock on the front door and returned to his parking patrol. I may have been the only person who was still watching when I ran to Buddy's car and climbed into his passenger seat.

*   *   *

My
Life

as a

girl

The heat in the Mustang was busted, sending out a whisper of warm breath as we circled the campus looking for a legal place to park. When Buddy braked suddenly at a stop sign, something heavy nudged my heels from under the seat.

"Great, Buddy, drinking and driving." I held up the frozen bottle of beer I'd retrieved.

"It's not open," he protested. He took the bottle from me and turned it in his hands. "Well, this is dead for sure," he said, and tossed it into the back.

"Get out," I said. "I'm driving. You probably haven't slept in days."

"I was hoping to catch up at your place," he said.

"First of all, I have a roommate," I said. "Second…"

Before I could name another reason why Buddy wouldn't be sharing my bed, he got out of the car and hustled around to the passenger side. I scooted into the driver's seat he'd made warm. "I'm taking you for some coffee," I told him.

"Any place that's got some heat."

Driving through Bryn Mawr, I realized for the first time how small a town it really was. Unlike Phoenix, it was completely knowable, with an old-fashioned town square and a string of mom-and-pop stores along the main street. It took one minute to get through it. I parked in front of a bread store locally famous for free samples. Its windows were steamy, beckoning with warmth.

"Here's the deal," I said as I handed Buddy a take-out cup of black coffee and a slice of raisin walnut, which he wolfed down. "I've got a Spanish exam tomorrow morning, and I haven't started studying. You can get cleaned up at the dorm while everyone's at lunch, but afterward you have to go."

"Spanish?" Buddy asked. "You came all the way out here to learn Spanish? You could have done that at home."

"This is Spanish literature," I told him. "Borges and Marquez and—Buddy, I'm not going to transfer to Arizona State."

"Did I *say* I wanted you to?" Buddy asked, spitting bits of bread. Behind the counter, the store owners looked up from the dough they were pushing around on a floured board, then, embarrassed to be eavesdropping, quickly looked down again.

I tried to whisper. "If you're not here to convince me to come home, then why are you here?"

"Why are *you*?"

Which was a question I cared not to ponder at the starting block of finals week. In the next five days, I had to write two ten-page papers and take exams in Spanish, physics, and anthropology. My brain was already stuffed full with formulas and facts and theories; there was no room left for any question that would not appear on these tests.

"I know you're mad I didn't tell you I was leaving," I said. "I was going to." I didn't say it, but I was

My
Life
as a
girl

thinking, *The day you were hauled off by the Phoenix police.*

"What—you couldn't call?" he asked. "You couldn't write a letter?"

"I've been busy," I said lamely.

"Like I haven't been busy trying to find you!"

At that, the bakers stopped kneading and seemed to survey the distance between the counter and Buddy. "Calm down," I hissed.

"I have to explain what happened that day."

"Buddy, you don't. It doesn't matter."

"How can you say that," Buddy asked me, "when you ran away from me?"

"I didn't run away from you. I went to college," I said. I gulped my coffee and looked past him out the window, trying to read the thermometer that hung on the wall. "Besides," I muttered, "we were over, anyway."

Buddy got up angrily and crushed his empty paper cup. "I should have known you'd burn me!" he yelled. I imagined an echo: *Just like you burned your dad.* Six months in prison, and I hadn't visited. But Buddy didn't know that, did he?

He pulled open the door of the bread store and strode into the cold, bright day. Something—pride or shame—made me follow him, when I could have let him go. Still, like any girl brought up in Phoenix, I remembered my manners. "Thanks!" I called out cheerfully to the bakers, who waved nervously and went back to their loaves.

In the car, I stared out the window while Buddy fiddled with the heat. If the idea of us was ridiculous, so was living in a place where twenty-three degrees was "chilly," where natives called precipitation by a hundred different names. And yet, here I was, clear across the country on the day my father was going to be tried.

I said quietly, "Everything's different now, Buddy."

"I told you, those charges were bogus."

"I told *you*, it doesn't matter. My feelings for you have changed."

"Oh, yeah?" he said. He stroked my cheek. I could have stopped him, but I was curious. "Nah," he said after he'd kissed me. "You're still the same girl. You're just in a different place."

In the overheated room I shared with Amanda, I couldn't stop shaking. My teeth were banging together as I handed Buddy a clean towel and a new bar of soap. "The bathroom's down the hall," I said. "You've got twenty minutes to wash up before people start coming back from lunch."

But Buddy wasn't in a hurry. "What are you scared of?" he said, setting the towel and soap on my desk.

"I'm not scared."

"You're shaking."

"I'm cold."

My
Life
as a
girl

"Well, it's hotter than blue blazes in here," he said, throwing his jacket on the bed. He pulled out my desk chair and sat in it backward, as though he'd been invited to settle in. I stood by the radiator, which knocked furiously in rhythm with my chattering teeth. A tooth that had hurt off and on all semester shot pain through my jaw. I found a stick of gum in my coat pocket and put it in my mouth as a kind of jaw-stop.

"It's not like I pictured," Buddy said, eyeing Amanda's pale green comforter, elegant brass library lamp, the antique lace she had brought to cover her dresser.

"This is my roommate's side," I said.

Buddy said, "I figured that." Amanda inhabited her half of the room with confidence, the same settling-in instinct the other boarding school kids had.

My half of the room was a mishmash: old-fashioned patchwork bedspread, modern stretch-neck desk lamp, copper bookends shaped like saguaros, an *Arizona Highways* wall calendar featuring stunning photos that didn't remind me of home. I'd packed my steamer trunk so hopefully with these accessories to my new life, and I was glad to have them, though they didn't make me smarter or courageous or from a family as happy as Amanda's. The trunk itself, covered with one of my roommate's embroidered linen lap napkins, did make a decent coffee table, though.

I switched on the radio, tuned to Amanda's classical station, to muffle the sound of my unruly teeth.

"KJAM rocks," said Buddy.

"I like this," I said—"this" being not the orchestral piece in particular but the memory of hearing the Philadelphia Orchestra with Amanda and her parents. The music made me think of well-dressed patrons arranged in the Academy of Music's plush seats, the stage curtained in red velvet, the crystal chandelier as big around as a swimming pool.

"Whatever," Buddy said.

He got up and opened the door to Amanda's closet, which was full of noisy party dresses made of fabrics that rustled and jingled and squeaked. These were only warmups for the gown she'd wear at her "coming out" party at Christmas, an event she planned on the phone with her mother while braiding her hair and rolling her eyes.

"What do you need these for?" he asked suspiciously.

"Those are Amanda's," I said as he took out a black moiré cocktail dress. I added, as if the word would mean anything to him, "She's a debutante."

Buddy whistled. "Nice," he said.

Amanda had worn the dress the night we went to hear the orchestra, and afterward had accidentally flicked her cigarette onto the skirt and burned it. This flaw made the dress truly glamorous. Through that tiny hole in the fabric, I glimpsed the world of wealthy young adulthood, heard jazz and laughter and the tinkling of ice in highball glasses—an impression gath-

My Life *as a girl*

ered not from direct experience but from reading *The Catcher in the Rye*. Holden Caulfield had warned me that Amanda's world wasn't perfect; old money suffered tragedies and ordinary sadness, just as new poor did. Still, sometimes I wanted to throw my life in the hamper and put on Amanda's.

Buddy put the dress back in the closet and leaned against the door as he cased the room. "All this place needs," he said, taking out his wallet and pulling a photograph from the billfold, "is a picture of us."

"All I need," I said, chewing the stick of gum violently, "is for you to get cleaned up and get going, so I can study for Spanish."

Buddy laid the photo on my pillow, then sat down on the bed. If I squinted, he almost looked collegiate: a disheveled philosophy major, or a rugby player fresh from the field. When I widened my eyes, though, he came back into focus. I still couldn't quite believe he was here.

"I'll help you," he offered. "I'm pretty good at cramming."

"Or cheating."

He shrugged. "Whatever you need."

"Buddy, I mean it. Get going."

"Hold your horses," he said, but he hauled himself up from the bed, gathered the soap and towel, and followed me down the hall.

At the bathroom door, he paused again. "Are there chicks in here?" he asked, fidgeting with the bandage on his hand. He didn't want an encore with my hallmates, who'd be surprised—if they'd believed his wound was in earnest—to find Buddy alive and still hanging around.

"I hope not," I said. Still, I gave the customary warning knock before I pushed open the door. "Man coming in!" I called out. No answer; all clear.

I stood guard outside the bathroom, willing Buddy to hurry before lunch ended and my hallmates began to drift home. I wasn't breaking any rule by having him in the dormitory, but I was risking a reputation as weak and, worse, a fool. When Buddy finally came out, he was shirtless, toweling a wet head of spice-scented hair.

"Where'd you get the shampoo?" I asked.

"On that shelf by the shower," he said.

"Buddy—that's someone else's."

"Someone else left it out."

"We have an honor code," I said, leaning into the bathroom to look. Of course, he'd selected Melissa's. I put the shampoo bottle back in her cubby and made a mental note to replace what he'd used.

"People don't lock their stuff up?" he asked me. "This place is really wild."

I nudged him back to my room. "Don't get any ideas," I told him. "And put your shirt back on."

The phone was ringing as we entered. It was Amanda, calling to warn me she had to come back to the room to retrieve an art history book.

My
Life
as a
girl

"Is Buddy still there?" she whispered.

"He's gone," I said, and Buddy scowled. I scowled back. I hoped that by the time she made her way over from the library, this would actually be the case.

"Oh," she said, sounding disappointed. "Well, anyway, I'll be right up."

"Up?" I asked, but she had already disconnected. "It's my roommate," I told Buddy. "She's downstairs. We've got to hide you, quick."

My own closet was less full than Amanda's, as befitted my considerably lesser social life. On the floor a pair of barely worn cowboy boots stood stiffly like sentinels. I nagged myself for buying them every time I saw them, but I couldn't bring myself to throw them out.

Now I shoved the boots aside and packed Buddy in among the jeans and sweaters. "Please keep quiet," I begged him. "This shouldn't take long."

Amanda picked up the photo from my pillow and studied it as though it were one of the 200 paintings she had to memorize for her exam. "Oh," she said, "The Phoenix. I remember the letter you sent from that hotel."

The picture was taken at the pool's edge, where Buddy and I had posed as a couple in love. In it, I looked stunned, but he was grinning, wearing the hotel's logoed polo shirt. I took the picture from her and put it away in my desk drawer. "That was a huge mistake," I said, hoping Buddy would hear.

"Do you wish you hadn't?" Amanda asked, and I understood from her question that she believed I'd slept with him. It wasn't true, but I let her believe it. It was easier than explaining that though I'd held on to my virginity, I'd let him ravish the rest of my life.

"I guess not," I said, moving as far from the closet as possible, sitting on the edge of my bed. "I mean, how can you learn if not from your mistakes?"

I hadn't meant this as an invitation, but Amanda took it as one. She flopped down on her own bed, gathering her goose down pillow beneath her. I recognized this posture as a prelude to the activity that defined Bryn Mawr and illuminated the windows of our dorms and libraries late into the night. This place was full of women passionate about ideas, who loved more than anything to talk. And talk. And talk.

"John Locke wrote that all knowledge comes from experience," said Amanda, "that our ideas are formed from our senses. But if that's true, who are we but a collection of pictures? I mean, who arranges them in the album?"

I was so weary of talking, of analyzing every impulse and theory and situation under the sun. All semester, we'd argued about everything from the meaning of feminism to which of three silly lyrics we should choose for our class song. What I wanted, in that moment, was not to explore the principles of human understanding and identity, but to send

Amanda back to the library so I could get rid of the boy in my closet. "*I* arrange them," I said unenthusiastically.

"Why is it, then," she mused, "that we so often let our emotions lead us? Why don't we think before we act?"

I could have smacked her then, for looking so chaste and thoughtful as she presumptuously used the word *we*. What did she know of the hurt and longing that could drive a girl—I mean, *woman*—to love the wrong person? "Amanda," I said finally, "haven't you ever made a mistake?"

"Of course I have," she said. "That's not what I meant. I'm asking you, sincerely, if our power to reason can save us from our fate?"

I heard the contents of my closet shifting. "No," I said loudly, to cover the sound.

"Just no?"

"Am I taking an exam?"

"Of course not. But don't you think—"

"I think you can't spend your whole life thinking. Sometimes you just have to act." With that, I strode to my dresser and began brushing my hair, as if good grooming were the sole important statement I was on the earth to make.

"Maybe so," said Amanda. Which surprised me, since Amanda usually held fiercely to her opinions, even if they were mostly borrowed from books.

"Don't you have to study for art history?" I reminded her.

To my great relief, she stood up and lifted her hundred-pound Janson's *History of Art* from her bookshelf. But then she said, "I thought I'd just study here."

"You can't," I said.

"May I ask why?"

Good question. I had vowed that morning to be truthful about Buddy, but now found myself defaulting to a lie. "I'm getting ready to take Spanish," I said, holding up the sealed envelope in which my professor had placed the take-home exam.

"Already?" asked Amanda. "I thought you hadn't studied."

"Not as much as I'd like to," I said. "But I've wasted half the day with Buddy, and now I'm way behind."

I regretted mentioning him when Amanda set down the Janson's and pulled out her desk chair. She was perilously close to sitting. "Was he brokenhearted," she asked, "when you told him to leave?"

"Amanda," I said, "can we talk about this some other time?"

"All right," said Amanda, "I'll give you some space." She slid the book into her backpack, where it landed with a heavy, profound-sounding thud.

The door had barely closed behind her when Buddy spilled out of the closet, a stupid dog grin on his face. "Now you've made me lie to my roommate," I accused him. "I'm getting you out of here before you do any more damage."

My
Life
as a
girl

"Whoa!" said Buddy. "It's not my fault the chick decides to come home."

"She thinks I'm taking my Spanish exam," I said, waving the envelope at him. "She knows I haven't studied. She probably thinks I want the room because I want to use my books."

"So what?" said Buddy.

"That's cheating," I said. "The test is closed-book."

"Right," said Buddy. "Like everybody in your class isn't doing the same thing." He snatched the envelope out of my hand.

"Don't open it!" I warned him just before his finger sliced through the flap. I grabbed the envelope away from him and stuffed it safely into my coat pocket, out of my sight. "Damn it, Buddy!" I said. "You are out of here *now!*"

But before he could drive off into the sunset, Buddy insisted on fixing his heat. I leaned against the Mustang and drummed my fingers on the hood while he took apart the glove compartment, looking for the fuse.

Looking up, Buddy said, "You can go now."

"Not until you do."

Up close, I noticed ripples in the car paint, dead gnats and chunks of moths that had been caught in the hasty job. The sight made me sick, so I moved to sit on the icy curb.

I was trying to be patient. I wanted Buddy gone,

but I couldn't begrudge him a working heater in December. People froze to death in Pennsylvania—General Washington's soldiers, for example, just a few miles north at Valley Forge.

A chubby squirrel staggered past me, heading for the base of a maple tree, where he seemed to be stashing some nuts. "You're a little late for that," I muttered as he scratched the hardened ground. He dropped the nut in the hole he'd dug, then darted around to the left and to the right. The little dance was entertaining the first few times, but the senselessness of the ritual began to get on my nerves.

"Are you done yet?" I asked Buddy. My butt was almost numb.

Buddy slammed the glove compartment closed. "Not unless you've got a fuse."

"Buddy, you're not staying," I said, standing up quickly. "I'll give you a blanket, some mittens. Whatever you need to keep you warm."

"I need a new fuse," Buddy said bitterly. Still, he closed the door and turned the engine over. I was so relieved to see him going that, when he rolled down the window and beckoned, I would have forgiven him for everything, would have even kissed him good-bye.

Then Buddy reached out and hooked me roughly with his left arm, without even taking his right hand from the wheel. "I'm not through with you yet," he said. Just as suddenly, he released me, and I jumped back from the car. "Go," was all I could manage to say. My teeth were banging together as I turned to walk back to my dorm. I hadn't noticed until it started up again that the chattering had stopped.

The noise of the Mustang's wheels fighting asphalt frightened the squirrel I'd been watching, who now stood paralyzed in my path. He was clutching something; as I got closer, I could see he'd only made a show of burying the nut, while all the while he'd concealed it in his paws. I started to laugh at his trickery. Then I froze, as Buddy laid on the horn of the Mustang, letting it wail for miles and miles.

Someone had strung colored lights around one of Merion's windows, which flashed prettily in the smoky late-afternoon light. Seeing the display, I felt a surge of panic about Christmas. It had always been a weird holiday in our house, with Dad playing spendthrift Santa, Mom mentally tallying the damage. I never knew whether I should accept my gifts with gratitude or take them back to the store. This year Dad might not even be with us. Either way, it was going to be dismal.

In front of the dorm, a group of students were building a snowman. They looked like little mother-bundled kids playing in their bright jackets, their book bags abandoned on the sidewalk. I stopped to watch them for a moment, thinking that I had never seen such a beautiful sight. Why did I feel so sad then? What prevented me from joining in? My jaw ached. I was freezing. I had to study. Whatever the real reason, I trudged past them, heading for my room.

I climbed the stairs heavily, shedding my frozen mittens as I went. I thought of the uncompleted Woolf paper, the long line of exams—but behind these worries was another that I couldn't quite put my finger on. Ever since Buddy showed up, I'd had a feeling of moving backward, and now I felt as if I were wading upstream with weights tied to my feet. I shed my coat, draped it over my arm. I would have liked to drop it on the landing, lie down on top of it, and go to sleep.

"You lost something," said Amanda, behind me.

I turned and saw that the Spanish exam I'd stuffed into my coat pocket had worked its way out and fallen to the floor. She handed me the torn envelope, a puzzled look on her face. She must have decided to dismiss her suspicion, but in that moment when our eyes met, I knew that I was not only capable of cheating, but that I'd been on my way to do so, and would have if she hadn't interrupted me. She asked me cheerfully, "How did it go?"

I started crying then, really sniveling, right there in the hall. Amanda looked stunned and gave me a quick hug, saying, "You probably did better than you think." But her kind words only made me cry harder. "Is it Buddy?" she asked, and I shook my head. "Do you feel ill?" She was flailing. "Are you hungry? Do you need help with your paper?" Finally, she stopped guessing. She put her arms around me and let me sop the shoulder of her camel hair coat.

I had only ever cried in front of Rosa, and couldn't

believe that anyone but Rosa could ever understand. But Amanda was well practiced in offering comfort. She made me a huge mug of cocoa,
which I held against my throbbing jaw. She
offered to rub my shoulders, and showed me her
embossed leather photo album full of kids from
her boarding school. "Better?" she asked when I'd
stopped shuddering, and I nodded, though I knew that
I would never be the same. My sense of belonging at
Bryn Mawr was so fragile, and I had almost done
something that would smash it to smithereens.

I still had to get through exam week, and so, as I'd
learned to do in high school, I packed my shame away.
I didn't take it out again until exams were over and I
was on the plane back to Phoenix, suspended miles
over Bryn Mawr, over Buddy, beginning the long tra-
jectory home.

"Writing the Great American Novel?" asked the
man wedged into the seat next to mine. He'd already
introduced his elbow into my space, and now he cast
his eyes over the pages of my journal.

"Just notes," I said, glancing down at the lone
entry: 1. DON'T CALL BUDDY. I closed the notebook
quickly. There, on its cover, was the college logo.

"Ah, Bryn Mawr," he said, raising a fat pinky from
his plastic cocktail cup. "That's a girls' school." I nodded, trying to be pleasant, though my jaw burned and
I'd been up all night finishing the Woolf paper, which
I'd just handed in an hour before. I could tell he was

casting about for entertainment, diversion from the files waiting in his briefcase. I felt drained just watching him sit there, expecting to be served.

He took a sip of his drink and said, "Pretty fancy place."

"Pretty tough, too," I said, just the slightest edge in my voice. I had never worked harder in my life than I had at Bryn Mawr, except during the summer, when I'd had to work two jobs to earn enough to get myself there.

The man touched my arm and leaned in toward me, trapping me in a brown cloud of bad breath. "I bet the hardest part," he said, winking, "is living without men. I mean, what do you do for fun?"

"I've had plenty of fun," I said. I closed my eyes to get away from him, and leaned back against the head-rest to think. I needed to steel myself for the verdict that would be waiting when I got home. I remembered my father's careless games and those I had played with Buddy. I'd had so much fun it was a wonder I'd gotten to Bryn Mawr at all.

chapter

three

"No way are you wearing a bunny getup and taking money from drunks," my best friend Rosa warned me when I circled the ad for COCKTAIL WAITRESS WANTED. I'd only tried the idea on as a dare—you had to be twenty-one, anyway, to serve—but Rosa was serious. She snatched the newspaper away from me, rolled it up, and swatted me with it on the head. "You lose your clothes, girlfriend, you lose respect, too," she said. Rosa could afford to be uncompromising; she was guaranteed a summer job in her family's souvenir store downtown. The Gutierrez family took care of their own, while *my* dad took our savings to Vegas and left us to fend for ourselves.

It was the summer before Bryn Mawr, and my plan was to work two waitress jobs: one at The Phoenix, where a single night's tips would buy me *Gray's Anatomy,* and another at a greasy spoon. I'd take a day shift at the diner, a night shift at the pricey place, go back and forth between them. I thought I could pull it off.

I'd almost hooked the job at Ben Franklin's All-American Diner. I was smiling at the manager and leaning toward him, betting on his chubby face and straight, boyish bangs to make him behave, when he *winked* at me and said, "Under one condition."

I startled as if I'd been bit by a lapdog. It was early morning, and we were the only two people in the diner, alone in a vinyl booth, our knees nearly touching under the table. Though I hadn't wanted Mom to come with me to the interview, I was suddenly glad she was outside, waiting in our Pinto in the parking lot. I could see the car from where I was sitting, blue faded white from the Arizona sun. I hoped the manager could see it, too.

"What condition?" I asked, shifting my body toward the window.

"That you won't leave me in September," he said, setting my application aside. He had this dreamy smile on his face, and he was drawing voluptuous spirals on the steno pad he'd used to take notes. Glancing down, I saw him circle a word I hadn't noticed before: pretty.

Mom always told me I was lucky to be pretty, but Rosa had raised my consciousness. "Walk it like you talk it, if you want to go somewhere," she'd say.

"Listen, Mr. Thew," I said.

"Kenny," he corrected, tapping his nametag with his pen.

"Kenny," I said. I gripped the table's red-white-and-blue Formica rim to remind myself of the distance between us, space made for wideload truckers roaring in hungry off the Black Canyon Freeway. "What are you insinuating?" I asked, hoping the dirty-sounding word would make him back off.

But my accusation only dangled there between us, making *me* blush. Sure, I'd been flirting before, but couldn't he see I was just being polite?

Kenny leaned closer. "I know you college kids," he whispered as though we were conspirators.

"What do you know about us?" I asked, white-knuckling the table rim, ready to defend my morals.

He looked confused for a second and then said, "You're gone when summer's over, and I've got to hire all over again."

"Oh, *that*," I said, relieved he wanted only loyalty, and not to fool around in the walk-in fridge. I let go of the table, let out my breath, and was surprised to find that behind my relief was a ready-made lie. "I'm deferring a year," I lied, looking down at my application, the line that said EDUCATION, where I'd proudly written Bryn Mawr. I was honest enough to be ashamed to meet his eyes, but corrupt enough to know he would take it as humility. "To work for tuition," I added. "My financial aid fell through."

"That's rough," he said, sounding really concerned.

"It's not the worst thing that could happen," I said, and right away I was superstitious for my scholarship, which paid tuition while I worked for room and board and book money. Losing it *was* the worst thing I could think of. I was counting on college to change my life. I tapped the table's underside, wincing as my fingers hit chewing gum instead of wood.

"Can't anybody help you?" Kenny asked. "Your parents?"

I shook my head. I didn't tell him Mom worked for minimum in the bakery at El Rancho, and Dad was indisposed in prison, awaiting his trial for embezzlement. What if Kenny had seen Dad's picture in the paper, the headline calling him CAPTURED CON?

For a second, Kenny's pen quit scratching on the page. "Boyfriend?" he asked, looking up from his steno pad and right at my collarbone.

I should have known.

I should have told him, *Listen, mister, I've got myself to rely on, and that's plenty. Whose grades, after all, got her into Bryn Mawr?* That's what Rosa would have done. But if I'd learned one thing in eighteen years, it was how guys bow to the word *boyfriend*.

"He's saving up for an engagement ring," I said in an octave higher than my own, hardly believing what I heard myself say. There was no boyfriend, no promise of a ring. As Rosa would say, I wasn't going to college to get an M.R.S. It fooled Kenny, though. He coughed and said, "Okay. Gotcha. Loud and clear."

Then I worried the ploy had worked too well, that if I was already taken, Kenny would take back the job. I'm like my dad that way, can't walk away from the table when I'm winning. "In the meantime…" I said, rattling the ice cubes in my tea, "I'm staying in Phoenix."

My
Life

as a

girl

That lie came as easily as a habit. It was the first line of a rap called "Worst Case Scenario," which Rosa and I used to say. *I'm staying in Phoenix,* one of us would start, and together we'd make up a miserable life: hitched to some loser guy right out of high school, cramped into a trailer in Happy Tepee RV Park, selling fry bread with beans at the mall, drinking beer at desert parties. The game kept us from griping about busting our brains to get into good colleges, and geared us up to face the thin rejection letters we were sure we'd find in our mailboxes. Until that afternoon in April, when the fat packages containing letters starting "We are pleased..." came to us from Stanford, Rosa's first choice, and from Bryn Mawr.

"Isn't Bryn Mawr near Philadelphia?" Kenny asked, and I nodded almost imperceptibly, watching for some sign that I'd gotten the job. He patted my arm, as though in a second I'd gone from conquest to old flame. Then, slowly, he folded my application into quarters and tucked it into his breast pocket.

I waited, afraid to breathe, like a gambler watching the dice roll.

"I'm from back East myself," he said finally, and then went on about how people are friendlier in Phoenix, the usual stuff back-Easters say to flatter you, for what seemed like an hour. I listened and smiled and told myself the job was just my safety; I'd make bigger bucks at The Phoenix. But the more Kenny made me wait for the job, the more I felt I had to have it. I was almost as anxious as I'd been at my Bryn Mawr interview.

By the time Kenny had finally finished hyping about the laid-back western attitude, I'd blown the whole thing out of proportion. Suddenly, that job at Franklin's meant the difference between college or staying in Phoenix. Between my future as a doctor or being dependent on a man, like my mom. Between the M.D. degree I wanted and the M.R.S. that seemed a consolation prize.

"Can you start tomorrow morning?" Kenny asked.

"Yes!" I gushed, but then it was weird to have it decided. I felt more resigned to it than happy, the way my dad looked the time he won a pile at the greyhound races. That night he told me soberly, "You have to know your limit," as if winning were scientific and not just luck that could change in a minute, the way ours did.

Remembering Dad's words, I told myself I'd drawn the line, gone as far as I'd have to for a damn diner job.

Then Kenny said, "I'll go get your uniform."

"Army, navy, or marines?" I joked.

"I just love a girl in a uniform," he joked right back.

"Ha, ha," I said, tripping over the reprimand *woman*, which cowered at the tip of my tongue. That's what Bryn Mawr called its students, but in Arizona the line between one thing and another isn't so clear. I left it alone, but I was thinking: *This summer's the end of my life as a girl.*

My
Life
as a
girl

"Size small?" he asked, trying not to look at my body.

"Medium," I said, straightening up in my seat.

"Read up on the rules while I'm gone."

Kenny left me alone then with a heavy notebook called "Franklin's Almanac." On the cover was the same cartoon that glared out from the floodlit highway sign: long-haired Ben with his square spectacles flying an electrified kite, and beneath him a corruption of Poor Richard's famous words: "Live to Eat." I flipped through the plastic pages, skipping company policy to look at greenish photos of Franklin's seafood specials, revived and deep-fried versions of what people got fresh in Philadelphia. I'd seen pictures of a place called the Italian Market, where iridescent fish were laid out on ice, and live crabs scrambled around in buckets. But everything at Franklin's was hidden under greasy brown covers of breading, so you could hardly tell what anything was.

I shut the rule book and looked around the diner, trying to picture myself hurrying out of the kitchen with a Kite 'n' Key Krab Kake Platter, trying to picture ninety hot summer days of the same. Someone had tried to make Franklin's look like Philly, with faux-brick floor tiles and lampshades shaped like Liberty Bells. On the walls were sun-faded posters of Independence Hall and the Delaware River, both much cleaner than seemed possible, and an outdated picture of downtown, missing the newer, mirrored buildings I'd seen in Bryn Mawr's viewbook. This inside information made me feel smug for a minute. But then, imagining how I'd describe the diner to Rosa, I felt embarrassed by how it was done up as if it wanted to be somewhere else.

We'd always planned to go to Stanford together, right up until last fall. Maybe I chose Bryn Mawr instead because an Eastern women's college was as far from familiar as I could get. Or because, for the first time in my life, I wanted to go somewhere without Rosa.

Kenny returned from the back with a frilly white Betsy Ross blouse draped over his arm. "Is that your mother out there in the car?" he asked.

"She didn't want to come in," I said, glancing out the window to make sure. I thought she was afraid she'd make the wrong impression, spoil my chance to land this prestigious job. She must have been feeling optimistic, though, because the car windows were closed and the air was on, an extravagance at seven A.M. The old Pinto was shaking like a piggy bank coughing out coins.

A string of tiny Liberty Bells hanging from the door frame jangled a warning as Kenny leaned outside and waved her in. "Come in and have some iced tea," he called out, and I was surprised when she did.

As Mom came into the diner, I stood by the booth like a guard dog, ridiculous because Franklin's— believe it—was nothing you'd want to defend.

My
Life
as a
girl

"Please excuse my uniform," she said, more to me than to Kenny, as she ran a hand across her hair net like a spotlight calling attention to it. Her fingers were rainbow-stained with food color, and she had on her wedding band. Later in the day she'd remove it, complaining her fingers had swelled from forcing cake icing through pastry tubes. The plastic badge on her chest bore her maiden name, Johnna Wynn, which she'd recently taken to using.

At home, Mom dressed like all the women in our old neighborhood, wraparound skirts mail-ordered from Talbots, back East—so she still looked strange to me in her uniform. But Kenny took in the bakery apron, the hair net, and the stained fingers as though this was all there was to her. He'd fixed a smile on his face, like nothing she could say or do would surprise him. I thought how I'd give anything to keep a man from sizing me up that way.

But Mom just stood there in her uniform, a pretty-enough woman looking pleased to meet him. "I'll excuse your uniform," Kenny laughed, tugging on the sleeve of his short-sleeved dress shirt, a style people probably laughed at back East, "if you'll excuse mine."

Mom, of course, was charmed by this. "Nice place," she said as Kenny hustled away to pour her some tea, but she really meant *nice man.* I almost told her about the wet dreams this nice man had doodled on his steno pad, but by then I was doubting what I'd seen. I slumped back into my booth seat, which the air conditioning had turned clammy cold. Mom slid in beside me. "I bet you'll meet all kinds of neat people here," she said.

I scooted away a few inches. "You mean like truckers and drug runners?" I said, hating her persistent cheerfulness, the pioneer spirit I had always admired. No matter how bad things got, Mom still insisted we were lucky. And here I'd made up bad luck, the bit about the lost scholarship, to get a diner job. In Mom's book, a person couldn't go any lower than to trade pride for pity, and knowing that made me nasty. "Maybe we can start a book group," I said.

Mom said, "Remember, you're lucky to get that fancy education."

She meant Bryn Mawr. *I earned it,* I wanted to shout at her, but my life was still mixed up with hers; I wasn't sure what was mine to claim. I only knew what had been taken from me, and what I wanted to leave behind.

We'd been rich, and then one day, after Dad's boss called him in to question receipts from a "business" trip to Vegas, we weren't. I kept thinking we'd get back on our feet again, even while Mom sent our family room furniture back "for repair," "lost" our better car, and moved us from our house to an apartment "for the time being." After Dad was arrested, she stopped the newspaper. All that time, I believed she was keeping us safe, putting some distance between us and disaster. Now I thought she'd been protecting herself.

My Life *as a girl*

"It will be good for Jaime to work with real people," Mom told Kenny as he set down a sweating glass of tea and took a seat across from us. "Before she heads off to the ivory tower."

"Ivory tower?" Kenny asked.

"Bryn Mawr," Mom said proudly.

Hearing that word, I snapped to attention; I'd almost forgotten the lie that got me the job. By then I was so far in that admitting to Kenny that I *was* going to Bryn Mawr seemed as awful as Mom's catching me in a lie about it. I was scared Kenny would blow my cover. I felt like laughing out loud.

Kenny looked first at Mom, then at me. He opened his mouth and closed it, blinked at me once, and considered. "Who knows?" he said finally, clasping his hands behind his head and spreading his arms back, so his grinning face looked like a peacock's backed by its fan. "If Jaime's as good as she says she is, she might be my boss by the end of the summer."

"Who knows?" Mom laughed along, though she looked alarmed for a moment, picturing my career at the All-American Diner. Then Kenny winked at me so slightly it was almost a twitch, and it hit me that he thought he was protecting Mom from my bad news, the "lost" scholarship. When he handed me the Betsy Ross blouse and unfurled the skirt that lay beneath it, I knew he'd decided not to tell.

The skirt was the same faux-brick red as the floor and printed with white stars. It was cut as wide as a bell. I pictured my legs hanging from it, like a clapper.

"So chic," I said, trying to shrug off Kenny's complicity with sarcasm.

"Yes, very," Mom agreed.

You're staying in Phoenix, I could hear Rosa saying, *and you're wearing a Liberty Bell.*

Then Kenny said, "Of course, you'll have to hem it. Regulation is five inches above the knee."

"*Above* the knee?" I imagined my legs marked up like a ruler. The students I'd seen in the Bryn Mawr viewbook wore skirts hemmed between the knee and ankle, a dignified style with the quaint name "tea length." What Kenny was describing was more like beer length, a humiliating fashion that keeps coming back no matter how many women hate it.

"Regulations," he claimed.

Aha, I thought. I could hear Rosa saying, "How much are you going to compromise for two-o-one an hour plus tips?" I wondered myself.

Mom folded and pinched the material, frowning and clucking her tongue. "Five inches?" she asked, sounding uncertain. Surely she'd seen skirts that short in magazines, but those were made of tough denim or rich leather, not cheap muslin sprinkled with stars. On her face was the same blank expression I've used to shield myself on crowded city buses, not wanting to believe the hand that brushed my leg. I knew she was hoping he'd reassure her that his intentions were honorable, and I couldn't stand to watch her wait for it. "Is that really necessary?" she asked.

"It is at Franklin's All-American," Kenny laughed,

turning to me. "Is that a problem?"

"No problem," I said, without thinking. I was always trying to sound bold, like Rosa, to hide my fear of being found out or left behind. But Kenny saw right through me. "Deal?" He offered his hand.

I gave Kenny the firm handshake I'd practiced with Rosa for college interviews, but his palm was moist and yielding; his fingers curved around mine. He held my hand just long enough for it to occur to me that it was too long. I looked up, expecting a sly wink, but instead his face was gentle.

If I'd known I'd spend the summer fending off Kenny's fatherly kindness, I might have walked. But by that point in the interview, I was tired of trying to guess his game. "Deal," I answered, feeling reckless, the way my dad must have felt during that last binge in Vegas, when he went over his limit and bet his whole life.

"That's my girl," Kenny said.

I could see by the way Mom kept her head down, pretending to examine the uniform, that she'd decided to give Kenny the benefit of the doubt. Not out of innocence or generosity, but out of the necessary stinginess that comes from having nothing left but pride. I'd always believed that her trust in my father was as blind as a daughter's. But as I watched her fold and refold the skirt's material, measuring out the required hemline, I noticed how cautiously and deliberately she moved.

chapter

four

Even on the worst summer days, Rosa's house is always cool. While our brick apartment seems to beckon to the heat, sucking it in through the swamp cooler, the sun bounces off the Gutierrezes' adobe. Inside, the thick walls hold a family smell of meat cooking and cinnamon. I have always loved going there.

After my interview at the All-American Diner, I dropped Mom off at El Rancho and raced to Rosa's in the Pinto, pounding the scalding steering wheel impatiently, scowling into the nine o'clock sun. I parked at the curb and sprinted up the white-hot sidewalk path lined with prickly-pear cacti, toward the dark oak door. But before I could knock, Rosa's mother, Donna Gutierrez, pulled it open.

"*¿Qué tal,* Jaime?" she asked.

"Pretty good," I answered, and ducked into the entryway. In the sudden shade of the room, my eyes ached and I squinted like a mole. Odd colors floated before me, the familiar symptom of retina burn. "*¿Adónde va?*" I managed as Mrs. Gutierrez came

My Life

as a

girl

back into view from a cloud of green and yellow.

"I was just going to the store," she said.

"I thought you weren't open on Sundays," I said, disappointed to see that she was dressed for work, that by "store" she didn't mean the grocery, but La Piñata, the family business. The Gutierrezes usually had brunch together, after morning mass. While my parents recovered at home from Dad's night out at the greyhound races—he in bed with an ice pack, Mom at the table with the bankbook—I'd go to Rosa's and eat tortillas and eggs and spicy chorizo sausage.

But if there had been a feast here, it had already been eaten, the casseroles and dishes whisked out of sight. Mrs. Gutierrez was in a hurry, finger-combing her black broom of bangs, already halfway out the door.

"Our new mail-order business is really taking off," she answered, "and so Sunday's the only day I can do the books. Which reminds me…" She dug through her canvas bag and came up with a catalog. "I picked this up for your mother."

Our moms used to swap catalogs all the time—their Sears and Spiegel for our Talbots and "Needless Markup" (Rosa's name for Neiman Marcus)—but by then we had nothing left to trade. Mom had thrown away the few catalogs that kept coming since our credit cards were canceled, saying, "I can't believe all the trash in this world that's for sale."

But the catalog she handed me wasn't for dresses or even for La Piñata's turquoise rings and bolo ties; it was an application for Arizona State. I took it uncertainly. Though she'd written Mom's name on the label, I was afraid it was intended for me.

"Good luck with your test," she said, meaning the SAT of waiting tables I was to take at The Phoenix that day. She kissed my cheek, then "*Adios*, Rosie," she called.

"Velouté?" Rosa quizzed me from her room at the end of the hall, and for a second, I thought she spoke Spanish. Then I remembered the French cooking terms she'd been helping me practice. I answered, "Velvet puree."

"*¡Muy bien!*" Rosa said, and I could hear her sandals slap the terra-cotta floor tiles as she went about her room getting dressed. She'd offered to come with me to The Phoenix if I'd drop her off afterward at Saguaro Hospital, where she volunteered two nights a week and Sundays in the children's ward. "I'm almost ready," she said. "Come on back."

But I lingered a moment in the family room, my favorite place in their house. The Gutierrezes didn't live rich, but everything they had was old and elegant, well used but somehow preserved. The red hump-backed couch had once belonged to Rosa's grandmother Isabel Nieto. I rubbed my palm on the plush upholstery that was faded and flattened in places, and touched the mahogany armrests, worn pale and glossy

My
Life
as a
girl

at their wrists. Beneath the couch was a woven wool rug, sand-colored and striped with black, that always shocked me if I dragged my feet across it. And everywhere—sitting on window sills, resting atop the antique piano, hanging on the cream-colored walls—were photographs of family, the three generations of Nietos and Gutierrezes who'd lived in the same house.

"Paupiette?" Rosa called out around a toothbrush, above the sound of water running in the bathroom sink.

"Little cup," I said, without missing a beat. To show off, I added, "As in hollowed-out cucumber filled with salmon mousse."

"Papillote?" she asked, trying to trick me with a term that sounded similar.

"Package," I said smugly. "As in fish steamed in a paper wrapper."

"Braggadocio," she said, and I'd begun to translate the term into something edible when it hit me it meant: smart aleck. The word had appeared on the SATs.

"*Muchas gracias,*" I said.

I made my way down the hall slowly, admiring the series of silver-framed photos arranged in a line on the wall like a film strip. First, a view of the small orange grove the Nieto family had owned at Thirty-fifth Street, land that looked in 1930 like the end of the world. Then, pictures Rosa's grandfather Eduardo had taken, each a year apart, from the roof of the family's stucco-covered house. The photos showed the city creeping closer and closer, bringing houses and malls and ritzy mountain spas. Finally, they'd sold the orchard, bought a downtown storefront, and moved to the edge of a fancy neighborhood called Encanto Park.

Eventually Rosa's mother married and brought her husband, Elias Gutierrez, home; that's where Rosa and her sister Christina were born. Nowadays, the neighbors enlivened their bungalows and Spanish colonials with turquoise and raspberry paint, but the Gutierrezes' house remained traditional mission white.

There was a photo of the whole family in front of the house: grandfather Eduardo, Donna and Elias, aunts and uncles and cousins up from Tucson, Christina and Tina's husband, Tony, grandmother Nieto holding her namesake, baby Isabel. Behind them, the sagging arms of an old saguaro were draped with colored lights, and a sunburned plastic Santa stood guard by the door. The photo had been taken last Christmas, just before Dad's arrest.

Rosa came around the corner in her candy striper's uniform, twisting a tail of her long, mink-colored hair into a purple satin band. "I thought I'd find you here," she said, coming to stand beside me. I knew her family so well, had often wished they were my own.

I was looking at a photo of Tina's fifteenth birthday party, the *quinceañara* that Rosa had refused. In it, Tina wore a pink dress with a white sash and stood on the steps of St. Mary's, where her parents had once had to worship in the basement with others of Mexican

My
Life
as a

girl

descent. One of her white-gloved hands held a Bible, and the other shook the hand of the mayor, whose presence at the mass was recalled whenever the story was told.

Rosa had complained that the *quinceañara* was nonsense, more publicity for business than a celebration for her sister. Usually she scowled at the photo when she passed it, but today she blew dust off the cover glass and straightened the frame. Then she twirled in the peach aproned uniform she wore for her work at the hospital. "Here's my *quinceañara* dress," she said, laughing. "Much less expensive. Sweet, don't you think?"

"It's what all the candy stripers are wearing," I agreed.

"Ragout?" she quizzed me, wrapping an arm around my waist and pulling me to the front door.

"Gushy," I said, and winced as we stepped into the bright light outside.

"Gushy?" Rosa laughed, locking the door behind us. "I'd like to hear you say that to a customer."

"Whoops," I corrected myself. "I meant stewed."

"You should have seen the way he looked at me," I said, trying to rile Rosa about Kenny as we drove to The Phoenix. I wasn't testing Rosa so much as Kenny. I never knew what I could handle until Rosa checked it out.

But she wasn't having any of my complaints about Franklin's. "At least you're not cocktailing," she said as she pretended to tune the awful AM radio and fussed with the inoperable air-conditioning vent. "It's just one summer, Jaime. You'll be pouring tea for your calculus professor soon enough."

"And you'll be skipping class every time the surf's up," I kidded back. Rosa ignored me, pretending to be busy applying red lipstick in the sun visor mirror. "You missed the turn," she said.

"It's at Forty-eighth," I said.

"That was Forty-eighth."

"Where's the church?" I asked, pulling into the left lane to make a U. "Wasn't there a church on that corner last week?"

"It's condos now," said Rosa.

Phoenix was disorienting that way; people and houses and businesses came and went so quickly, making a familiar landscape strange. Turning, I said, "It's a wonder the mountains don't get up and move."

Ahead, Camelback Mountain had always marked East and, for me, a new start. I would cross those mountains in August, I remembered with a rush of relief. Secretly, I hoped that when I came home for Christmas, Dad's trial would be over and his criminal record erased.

"Is this your uniform?" Rosa asked me, pulling the bell skirt from my backpack.

"I have to hem it five inches," I told her. "Practically to my navel."

"Five inches?" Rosa asked.

"That's the rule," I said.

My
Life
as a

girl

Rosa unfurled the uniform and spread it across her lap. "Here's what you do," she said. She scrunched up the material, so the skirt looked even skimpier on her long legs than it would have on mine. "Follow the rule for the first week. Don't sew it, but fix it with tape. Then, little by little, let down the hem."

"That'll never work," I said.

"By the time this Kenny notices, he'll be so impressed with your work that he won't even care." Rosa pretended to tear the hem out, faking a juicy ripping sound.

"What if showing leg is my work?"

"Make him put it in your job description."

"Rosa!"

"Then quit and take my job at La Piñata."

"Take your job?" I asked, as surprised by her suggestion as I was by how much the idea appealed to me. Easy money, happy family—I would have gladly traded her place for mine. "But you're doing so well," I said. "Your mom told me the mail-order business is really taking off."

"Oh, yes," said Rosa sarcastically. "We'll make sure no tourist leaves without a beaded fringe vest or an ashtray shaped like Arizona!"

"What's up with you, Rosa?"

"Nothing," she said, but that word was just the cork for her bottled frustration. It turned out her supervisor at Saguaro had asked her to help run a peer sex ed program for "high-risk" teens, a polite word for kids from poor or violent or drug-dealing neighbor-hoods. Rosa had said "yes" immediately. But just that morning, her mother had said "no."

"Maybe she's afraid you'll learn something," I tried to joke.

"*¡Qué lástima!* I'm not a child!"

"Maybe she doesn't like the neighborhood," I suggested.

"The barrio, that's right," Rosa said, rolling her eyes. She unlocked her limbs, and flailed her arms in the air. "They want to pretend such poverty doesn't exist!"

"Maybe," I said. "But probably they just miss you already." I glanced at the A.S.U. application that lay on the dashboard, wondering if my mother was feeling the same thing.

Rosa didn't answer, but as we drove on, I saw her face soften and her hands refold neatly in her lap. It was the peacekeeping posture she'd put on for her parents ever since the letter came from Stanford, beckoning their last child away.

As I turned into the driveway for The Phoenix, the A.S.U. application tumbled to the floor. I bent to retrieve it, trying not to swerve. What was Mom up to? Was she hatching a plan to keep me home until Dad's trial? I tossed the application into the backseat, convinced that the lie I'd told that morning was turning into truth.

chapter

five

The road to The Phoenix is a winding rift through a golf course, landscaped with brittlebrush and burnt-orange birds-of-paradise. We entered doing twenty, as resort etiquette required. Two men hoisting golf bags paused in their rounds to smirk at my luxury sedan. I have to say I was glad to see their light faces stinging pink despite their big-brimmed sports caps.

"Must be from the East," Rosa teased. "They don't have enough sense to come in out of the sun."

"Don't be prejudiced," I said, playing on my new geographical alliance, though secretly I agreed.

Phoenix, my hometown and the hotel, got its name from a bird in Egyptian mythology that died in a fire and rose up from its ashes, immortal. People say the story inspired the pioneers who came to the city to start their lives over.

I think it must have scared them, too. Rather than take the desert on its own terms, they sprinkled down the dust with borrowed river water and built houses with porches to keep out the light. They learned to rely on ice and, later, air conditioning as a diver does oxygen. They respected the sun's force, if only because they feared its effects.

But Eastern visitors, vainly thinking the sun tamed, jog in triple-digit heat, tan their skin to rawhide, then resurrect themselves in the hotel swimming pool. It's the water that keeps the myth going, I thought, as the road curved again and the resort, a huge Aztec condo built into a mountainside, came into view. The Phoenix, prettied with improbable fountains and miles of thirsty lawns, is a monument to hope, or maybe denial.

"It's ugly," said Rosa.

"At least it shows we're not a cow town," I said.

We parked in the underground garage and entered the lobby by elevator. The doors opened onto a sand-colored room—not sand-sand like the carpet at Rosa's, but pinky-sand, as if the lobby had been swabbed with makeup made for pale complexions. In the room's center, a fountain overflowed in an orderly way from basin to gutter, in glittering crystal strands.

"How does it fall so perfectly?" I asked admiringly, as Rosa and I approached it.

"It's an illusion," she explained, guiding my hand to the nylon harp strings that kept the water on course.

"Wow," I said, letting the water stream over my fingers.

She was unimpressed. "I've seen it before, in the Tiki Room at Disneyland," she said. I could tell the place really bugged her. Either that or she was pouting about the argument she'd had that morning with her parents.

My
Life
as a
girl

"Good morning," a hostess announced from out of nowhere. She'd surprised us like a palmetto bug discovered in the bread drawer, the soft carpet muffling her stiletto-heeled steps. She glared at us with shiny eyes. An antenna of hair hung loose from her upswept cylindrical canister. "Welcome to The Phoenix," she said.

I tried to place her accent. Finally I crammed it into an unwieldy box in my brain labeled "Midwest." "Thank you," I said, though the hostess was staring at Rosa's dark skin and striking profile. I was used to that. Rosa was beautiful when she was in a good mood; in a bad mood, she was stunning. Beside her, I often felt overlooked.

"*Gracias,*" Rosa said.

"May I help you find where you're going?" the hostess asked.

Destination, I would learn, was of utmost importance at The Phoenix. Management tried to keep people moving, maybe to keep them from noticing how flimsy the place was beneath the bright paint.

"We're not staying here," I answered right away, as if to reassure her. "We've come for an employment exam."

"Let's see," she said, drawing a blunt fingernail across a floor plan she'd produced from the air. I stared at the paper, mesmerized. On the hotel grounds were five pools of various sizes: some with slides, some with saunas, some with cabanas. I saw myself claiming a lounge chair by the water, sipping a fruit drink, waiting for a boy whose face I couldn't quite imagine.

"Housekeeping is located by the Sonoran pool," the hostess recited with the false concern of a flight attendant pointing out safety features on a plane.

"We're not here to scrub toilets, if that's what you mean," Rosa snapped at the hostess, yanking me out of my reverie.

"Rosa!" I said, but I really couldn't blame her. If history mattered to anyone in Phoenix, Rosa's family would be royalty, like the Mayflower folks in the East. But I was going to work here, and I wanted my first day to go well. I wished she would just cool it. "I have a position in the restaurant," I explained.

The hostess rolled her eyes and dragged her finger back across the map, tapping a space a floor above, next door to the ballroom. "Right here," she said, frowning. "I suggest you take the stairs."

Then, "May I help you?" she swooned to the real customers, a well-to-do couple wearing tennis whites, who stood blinking and bewildered in the lobby after coming in from the sun.

Rosa got there first. She yanked open the gilded door, revealing an ash-gray cinder block stairwell. The Phoenix, for all the grandeur of the lobby, was ugly behind the scenes. Rosa didn't say a word as we went up the stairs, but there was attitude in every slap of her sandals.

"So what?" I said, but Rosa didn't answer.

My
Life

as a

girl

"Probably her hairdo's giving her a headache."
Rosa kept her angry silence, but I knew what
she was thinking. When we got to the restaurant, she waited with crossed arms in the foyer
while I was ushered in.

The test was proctored by a woman named Ms. Pickett,
who had a birdlike body and tiny, jeweled shoes. She
directed me and about ten other new employees to
champagne satin ballroom chairs that waited at tables
stripped of their linens. After she had passed out the
tests, we plucked bare her bouquet of stubby pencils
and began.

Studying for The Phoenix exam, I'd learned all
kinds of odd things were edible: medallion of buffalo
(weren't they federally protected?), roast saddle of
baby lamb (there ought to be a law!), stuffed breast of
pheasant (was there enough room for stuffing?).

Even the terms for preparation were foreign to me.
Meat at The Phoenix was almost always steamed and
grilled, and although several entrées were actually
fried in a skillet, you were never to utter the word. "Say
instead: browned or braised," the employee manual
commanded. Say *"carbonnade de boeuf,"* the Belgian
term for the hobo steak Mom made. Say "beverage" for
drink, except the alcoholic kind, which was not a drink
or even a cocktail, but a mysterious "something from
the bar."

Nothing at The Phoenix, not even the checks-
which-were-not-bills, was called by its real name.

Once I had mastered that logic, passing the test was a breeze.

Rosa met me outside when I'd finished, a sarcastic smirk on her face. As we descended the stairs to the lobby, she said, "Some dude from New Jersey was wandering around wearing brand-new chaps going, 'Ballroom? I thought this was the bull room!'"

"Right, Rosa," I said.

"Poor guy was looking for an authentic rodeo."

"Uh-huh."

We used to laugh about the city's five-star boastings: dude ranches in the hellishly hot desert, spas that were like high-priced boot camps, grotesquely glamorous hotels. But just then, flushed with passing and intoxicated by the excessive elegance around me, I was annoyed by Rosa's kidding. I felt too optimistic about the fortune I'd make at The Phoenix to join her in making fun.

"Even if I wanted to work here, I couldn't," Rosa declared.

"You're just mad because that hostess had me cleaning toilets," I accused. "I'm the one who should feel dissed."

"She didn't mean you, she meant me," Rosa protested. "The dark one with the domestic-help ancestry. Didn't you see how she thought she had me pegged?"

"You're exaggerating," I argued, pushing open the stairwell door.

My

Life

as a

girl

"Exaggerating? She practically put the apron on me."

"You're wearing an apron already," I said, referring to her candy striper's dress. "Maybe she just made an honest mistake."

"Please," Rosa said, rolling her eyes.

We exited by accident on a guest room floor, numbered one, instead of two, in the European way. The decor was the same pinky-sand as the lobby, and this unvaried color plus the constant hum of vacuum cleaners made the hall seem endless, a tedious tunnel demarcated only by numerous housekeeping carts. "Disneyland," Rosa muttered, and I had to agree. For some reason, I wanted to run the length of the carpet and bang on every door, to write my name on the walls with purple spray paint.

"This place is just begging for graffiti," Rosa said.

"Good thing I know you're kidding." Rosa hated how Chicanos were blamed every time a building got tagged.

"How do you know I'm kidding? Anyway, the maids would have to clean it up."

Heading toward the exit at the end of the hall, we passed a cart heaped with towels, trash bags, and cleaning supplies. On a lower shelf beneath these was a carton full of chocolate coins that Housekeeping placed on bed pillows, embossed on one side with a phoenix bird, on the other with Good Night.

Maybe to show Rosa we were still on the same side, I grabbed a handful of the coins and dropped

them into my skirt pocket. It didn't seem like
stealing, now that I belonged.

"Stop it!" Rosa scolded in Spanish. "What
makes you think you can take what's not yours?"

"Chill, will you?" I said, and sniffed my fingers for cocoa, though the scent was well sealed
behind tinfoil. I kept walking, the coins in my pocket
bumping and skidding against my leg.

But Rosa had stopped in the middle of the hallway
and planted her feet near the cart. "*¡Para!*" she
insisted again.

"Forget it," I tried, but that only made her madder.
When I turned to face her, she began speaking faster
and faster in Spanish until her words were not words to
me but a single, drawn-out note. I retrieved the coins
from my pocket and tossed them underhand onto the
cart, where they landed on a soft pile of freshly laun-
dered towels.

As Rosa and I stood there glaring at each other, a
woman appeared in the doorway. She was Mexican,
and she wore The Phoenix's flared and sharp-collared
housekeeping smock. Like my mom's uniform, hers
was tight in all the wrong places, and its brown-mus-
tard color emphasized the yellow tone of her skin.
Draped over her arm was a towel and a piece of silky
material, some other person's intimate apparel she'd
retrieved from the floor.

"*Lo siento mucho,*" I said, thinking my theft had
alerted her. The coins were scattered on a towel right
in front of her, gold and conspicuous, on a field of

My

Life

as a

girl

royal blue.

My apology surprised her. It hadn't been my prank, but the Spanish that had brought her out into the hall. She glanced at me quickly and then looked to Rosa.

"Buenos días, señorita," she said in a tone that dipped low like a curtsy as she took in the Chicana with the soft leather sandals and hammered silver earrings.

Rosa, who to me had always been larger than life, seemed unnerved by this woman's gaze. *"Buenos días, señora,"* she said, stepping backward. She blushed and raised her hands to her earrings as if to conceal their glitter.

That day, I saw Rosa for the first time at a distance, in relief against the Mexican maid. There, in my friend's yellow-brown skin, was the wealth of Mexico's Spanish conquerors but also the Indian's broad features, the part her family tried to deny. Rosa's parents had worked hard, against the city's old prejudice, to make it, and they wanted their daughter to run with the winners. As I watched Rosa take her hands from her jewelry and turn to walk on, I understood that her rebellion could only go so far.

The maid smiled at me and nodded, then went on with her work, stuffing the towel she'd carried into a laundry bag and gathering a stack of fresh linen. She caught the coins in her palm as they slid from the pile.

"¡Qué lío!" she sighed—what a mess!—and turned to reenter the room.

chapter

six

If at The Phoenix everything was served in a rich sauce of French syllables, at Franklin's All-American Diner dishes such as Washington's Crossing Fish-and-Chips, Stars-and-Stripes Shrimp, and Melting Pot Chowder were boiled down to vowelless acronyms—F/C, SS, MPC—as if any hint of patriotism had been allowed to escape in the steam. Franklin's founders intended the menu to be cuisine qua history lesson, and so had given common entrées Revolutionary names. But no matter what the menu said, the waitresses translated entrées to codes on their order pads. And side dishes—hush puppies, coleslaw, or platter (everything)—went down in history without fanfare as pups, slaw, or PLT.

At Franklin's, unlike at the Phoenix, there was no glossary of terms to study, no weed-out test to take. You learned the language by speaking it and earned the job by doing it. My first day, I shadowed an older waitress named Shelly as she cruised through a station gerrymandered by her regulars' favorite booths. I tried not to trip on my own feet as I chased her from table to table, listening to her banter with these people, trying to take it all in.

"How's that no-good husband treating you?" she asked various women, winking or frowning depending on the accuracy of the adjective. "Honey, this is no place to be on a diet!" she stage-whispered to an overweight man.

I winced every time Shelly opened her mouth, thinking for sure she'd upset or offend. But these folks seemed to appreciate her directness. In the time it took to serve lunch, coffee, and dessert, they offered their troubles and took her advice, encouraged by her willingness to listen and by her inability to be surprised.

Back in the kitchen, she shouted out their orders— "F/C and slaw, SS and pups/w.d. (well done)"—and taught me some other terms, too:

1. "Suggest-sell" ("Some coleslaw with that?").
2. "Boost the bottom line" (recommend the most expensive items).
3. "Diving for change" (groveling for tips—"Yessir, nossir"), something Shelly disdained.

She wasn't above subterfuge, though, to bring in a few extra quarters. She advised me to glue a picture of a baby—anyone's—to the bottom of my tip tray, so customers would dig deeper into their pockets. "Heartbreaker, huh?" she asked me, flashing her tray to show me a little boy about eight with bangs and an overbite.

I thought she must have clipped it from a magazine; she seemed too old—Mom's age—to have a kid that young. But "That's my Buddy," she told me, and tucked the tray into her pocket before charging through the kitchen door, two plates caught in the clamped jaws of her fingers and two balanced in the crook of her outstretched arms.

I followed her into the dining room, barely able to catch my breath before we loped back into the kitchen. Her path was a racetrack between the two places.

When Shelly was on, she was "traveling," and when harried, "in the weeds." But on or off, she sprinted back and forth in high-top Converse sneakers, her Monroe-white hair spritzed into a helmet, her lips a jagged two-tone where she'd chewed away the color.

"Give me Washington extra crispy and Betsy-on-a-bun," she called to Estevez and the prep cook Mark as she slapped the ticket on the order wheel. "Boys, I'm traveling today," she added. Shelly had two speeds: hurry and hurry up.

She had the same breezy attitude toward her personal life, performing it for regulars like stand-up comedy. "Call the authorities!" she said when a customer asked after Buddy. "His father checked out a long time ago, and I'll be damned if I know what to do with that boy."

It turned out the "boy" was eighteen, which meant

**My
Life**

as a

girl

Shelly had been pulling the tip-tray trick for a decade. From what I'd overheard, his antics were less than adorable. He'd dropped out of high school, wrecked her car, spent a night in jail for disturbing the peace. And that was just in the last six months.

Though I couldn't help but listen every time she spoke his name, the way Shelly blabbed about Buddy to customers bothered me. I hadn't told anyone but Rosa about my dad going to jail. I was so used to covering up for Dad—calling his hangovers "flu," his gambling "a hobby"—that I wouldn't have even known where to start. I wasn't even sure I could say it. Rosa said I should be angry, but when I checked my anger channel, it showed nothing but static and ghosts.

I think I liked Shelly because she was as unsentimental as a prickly pear, a self-proclaimed "fact maniac."

"Kenny said it was restaurant policy?" she scoffed when I complained about the five-inches rule. "Baby, he can take you to court, but there's no such policy in the Franklin's rule book. He's just hoping your legs will bring in some business."

"Then why's your skirt so short?" I asked.

"'Cause my legs are God's gift," she said, laughing. "But that's none of Ken's concern."

We were sitting together at our lunch break, sharing a pile of unidentifiable deep-fry. I poked through the fry pile, trying to locate a shrimp, but wound up instead with a mass of clinging clams.

"Clam?" inquired Shelly, as I spit out a mouthful less than elegantly into the red-and-white-striped napkin. "You can tell the clams by weight," she offered. "When they're clumped together, those bad boys weigh a pound apiece."

"Thanks for the tip," I said.

"Kenny says you're saving up to go to college in Philadelphia year after next," Shelly said, and I nodded, not wanting to lie out loud.

"Well, don't believe that Liberty Bell business," she told me, dipping something long and thin and fried in cocktail sauce and waving it before me like a baton. "That bit about ringing in freedom across the land. Some damn writer made that up a hundred years later. Sure, a few people rang cowbells, and you bet some idiot men fired guns at the sky. But I read in this book that the declaration was a disaster. People stayed home with their doors closed, scared of what would happen when the boss found out."

Maybe it was her hundred-mile-an-hour voice, or sitting down after running all morning, or the way she waved that saucy baton while I contemplated a lunch made of cornmeal and grease. Whatever it was, listening to Shelly was exhausting. A summer of double shifts stretched out ahead of me, and already I felt as if I'd walked a hundred miles.

"That can't be true," I protested. "That's like saying Betsy Ross didn't make the flag."

"She didn't," said Shelly, popping the whole baton into her mouth, then pulling a shrimp tail back through her teeth like a magic trick. "True fact," she said, unflustered. "Her grandson started that story. Sweetie, do you believe everything you read?"

"No," I said defensively. "I don't believe those stories you tell about your son."

"About Buddy? How's that?"

I thought better of it, but added anyway, "I think it's like the tip tray, a trick to get their sympathy."

"Wish I'd thought of that," Shelly said, snapping the elastic neckline of her Betsy Ross blouse. Then she turned serious. Grabbing me by the elbow, she promised, "He's a good boy," sounding as sober as Mom when she talked about Dad. "He just needs someone to remind him, is all."

"I've heard that before," said Casey, coming in from the dining room, her arms full of half-empty ketchup bottles. She unscrewed the caps and balanced them mouth to mouth on the table, letting one set of bottles drip to the other.

"Hush, Casey," said Shelly. "No one's asking you."

Then Shelly whipped out a current photo from her billfold and gave it to me. Buddy was good-looking: pool-blue eyes, hair combed smooth with one loopy bang begging for a hand to brush it back, straight, white (and, now I knew, partially artificial) teeth. Probably got his way with every female in the valley, starting with his poor old trusting mom. Good boy? Forget it. Look up *trouble* in the dictionary, and he'd be Figure 1.

When I gave the photo back to her, Shelly was scrutinizing me the way some parents do our menu, searching for nutrition while their kids screamed for the hot dogs we called Redcoats or a main course of French fries.

"I could introduce you," she said. "My car's in the shop, so he's picking me up."

"No, thanks," I said, taking a gulp of iced tea. "I've got two jobs this summer and—"

"You have to have fun sometime."

"Buddy's too much fun for Jaime," Casey said, sauntering to the table, looking me over the way a lover would. She seemed puzzled by my straight hair parted in the middle, and snickered when she reached my bright white canvas tennis shoes. "Unless," she said, grabbing a stack of trays and bumping backward through the kitchen door, "your idea of fun is dinner at the county jail."

The word *jail*, not surprisingly, made me breathe in my tea. Shelly slapped me on the back while I coughed the liquid out of my windpipe.

"He's a sheep trapped in a wolf's clothes," she said, when I'd stopped.

I tried another tack. Narrowing my eyes and lowering my voice to a level I hoped would hint at danger, I said, "I prefer the real thing."

"The real sheep?" said Shelly.

"The real wolf."

Shelly laughed so hard she forgot her greasy fingers and used them to wipe the joke-tears from her eyes. "Sweetie, I'm sorry, but you wouldn't know a wolf if he bit you on the nose."

"Oh, yeah?" I snapped back at her. I hate to be laughed at, can't stand to be teased. "My dad was arrested for embezzlement. I'm not as naive as you think." I waited, but Shelly's face didn't change. Then I said, "He took my college money, this account we called the Future, and lost it gambling."

Just like that, the awful truth was out. And it didn't turn to vapor as nightmares do when you tell them, but instead took on a monstrous life of its own. My life. Telling was like stepping back into a self I'd left for dead, feeling my stone-cold heart begin to beat again. I was afraid I'd look up and see *that* Jaime in Shelly's eyes.

But Shelly just reached across the table to pat my trembling hand. "That's your dad's debt, baby, not yours," she said. She put the photo of Buddy back into her purse.

Kenny came into the kitchen then from his cubbyhole office, jangling his huge ring of keys. I swear he blushed when he saw me. "Hey there, Jaime," he said, crab-walking sideways while he tucked in the tail of his shirt. "How's your first day going so far?"

His fidgeting was contagious; I tugged my skirt at the hemline to cover my knees. "It's a blast," I said, and a look of alarm crossed his face. I thought it was my answer, but then I realized he'd dropped the keys he'd been palming down the back of his pants.

When people do stupid things, I'm always embarrassed for them. So while Kenny was bit in the butt by his keys, I had to pretend it wasn't happening, grab my fork, and get busy picking apart a glob of fried clam. But Shelly, as usual, had to call him on it. "Straighten out your leg, babe, and shake it," she advised. The woman had no shame.

The keys jangled their way down Kenny's pant leg and landed on the floor. Then he took a step backward and crunched them with his foot.

"It's Jaime's skimpy uniform that's got you so shook up," Shelly said to Kenny, winking at me. "It's doing the same thing to the customers. Good Lord! I had to perform the Heimlich maneuver five times today."

Kenny cleared his throat then, just to make a sound to fill the space. I raised my fork to my mouth to fill it, and chewed and swallowed the dreaded clam.

"Like I was telling Jaime," Shelly went on, grinning at me, "there's a whole pile of skirts in your office. I'm sure we can find one that fits."

When he did speak again, Kenny's voice was a full octave deeper and a few notches louder. "Help yourself," he said to Shelly, tossing her the keys.

"Help myself?" Shelly said, springing up from our table to open the office door. "Lord, how about tens and twenties?"

"She's a real jokester," Kenny said, still careful not to look at me, now that my skirt had been certified obscene.

Shelly emerged with a new skirt a moment later,

this version much longer and brighter than mine. "Ta-da!" she cried, balling it up and launching it through the air to me.

"Thanks," I said shyly. I placed the skirt in my lap like a napkin. The extra inches of coverage made me feel bold.

"So," said Kenny, recovering his managerial tone. "What I came out to tell you is we're eighty-six on cabbage. I'm making a grocery run."

"Eighty-six?" I asked.

"Eight-six, rhymes with nix, means we're out," Shelly instructed, as she turned to write the number on the chalkboard next to the kitchen door. "Means we'll have to push puppies until Kenny gets back."

"Right," I said, though I'd never heard the term. I couldn't imagine running out of anything at The Phoenix, where a team of male chefs in pleated paper hats set out plates of food they'd artfully arranged.

"Keys, Kenny," Shelly called as he was halfway out the door.

"Yep," he said, as though he hadn't forgotten. Oven air from outside rushed into the room as he turned and fielded Shelly's underhand toss. "Back in a flash," he called out, and limped off into the parking lot, the ring of keys protruding from his pocket like a brass-knuckled fist.

Shelly turned back to the chalkboard and drew, alongside "eighty-six," a stick figure in a short-sleeved dress shirt and bolo tie. For a head, she gave him a smiling, whole cabbage. "Not so smart," she said, "but I'll give him points for sincerity."

"Eight-six, eighty-six, eighty-six," I chanted softly while she drew. I liked the sound of it: over, gone, done with. If only getting over your past were that easy. After telling Shelly, I was determined never again to admit what Dad had done. When I left for school in August, I planned to leave *that* Jaime, the poor girl who'd been duped, behind.

"Please don't tell Kenny what I told you," I said. "The last thing I need is his sympathy."

"That goes without saying," said Shelly. She put the chalk down and wiped her hands clean on her apron.

chapter

seven

The trip from Franklin's to The Phoenix took twenty
minutes by car, just enough time at stoplights to wipe
the fish grease from my fingers, recoil my hair into the
requisite bun, kick off my sneakers and step into bal-
lerina flats, pull the restaurant's slim black skirt on
over my head, and peel the diner's bell skirt off from
underneath it. At The Phoenix, in the dark of the
underground parking lot, I'd change my blouse from
Betsy Ross to button-down and emerge from the Pinto
transformed. Then I'd sprint up the parking ramp,
through the employee entrance, and clock in, panting,
with two minutes to spare.

That was on a good day.

But on Friday of my first week, I clocked out at
Franklin's and staggered to my car. When I tried to
start the engine, the Pinto responded the same way I
felt: its first enthusiastic gasp turned to a sputter as the
engine choked itself on its own gasoline.

"No, please, not today," I pleaded with the battered
old car. I tried to pretend it wasn't happening, told
myself that if I suffered for two minutes without air

conditioning, I could will the engine to life. I closed my eyes and sat there counting, while my clothes sponged up sweat from my skin.

When I couldn't stand the heat any longer, I turned the key again. The engine made a horrible sound, as if its insides were being scraped. Then the heart of the car we'd had since I was a baby—since my parents were barely grown up themselves—gave up, flopped to a stop, and died.

I looked at my watch. I had fifteen minutes. "I can't believe this is my life!" I wailed, resting my forehead on the scalding steering wheel. "Ouch!" I shouted, and checked the rearview mirror. The burn was less dramatic than I'd expected: a slash of pink welt rising just above my right eyebrow.

The boom-boom of a stereo sounded then, moving like an angry god's thunder across the parking lot. Suddenly, my rearview was filled with the nose of a charging white Mustang, which came to bounce on its brake in the place next to mine.

Buddy, I thought, glancing over at the boy in the gray felt Stetson who was stroking the steering wheel and looking at me. So far that week, I'd been fortunate to leave Franklin's before he arrived to get Shelly. My luck had just run out.

Desperately, I tried the ignition, straining to hear my engine against his blaring steel guitar. Suddenly, the music was gone and there was only the embarrassing *click* of my car's failed heart. I tried three more times: *Click. Click. Click.*

My
Life
as a
girl

Rap. Rap. Rap. Buddy was crouched at my window, grinning and blinking a black net of lashes over his pool-blue eyes. He wound his fist in the air, a signal to roll down my window. From behind the glass he mouthed words I hoped and feared were: *Can I help you?*

The window's hand crank was broken. I swung open the door.

Buddy jumped back. I knew that I'd misread his lips behind the window glass when the first thing I heard was, "You have to go out with me."

"Wrong," I said, pushing past him. "My car won't start. I've got to use the phone."

"Hey, need hauling somewhere?" he called after me. "I'm free."

At the pay phone, I was punching out our number when I realized Mom was, at that moment, on the bus traveling home. I thought of Rosa, but she worked at La Piñata until seven, and besides, she didn't have her own car. Obviously, I couldn't ask Dad. I'd call a cab, I decided, hefting the phone book and bunching through its torn and folded pages. So I'd have to spend my Franklin's tips on the fare. At least I'd save face at The Phoenix.

"Half-hour," barked the dispatcher at Road Runners.

"I can't wait that long," I whined. "I'm late as it is."

"It's rush hour," he said, taking pleasure in the fact. "Call another company. They'll tell you the same thing."

I slammed down the phone and turned and marched back out the door. *It'll start now, it'll start now, it'll start now,* I chanted on the way to the car. My shadow on the pavement was ridiculous: stiff shoulders, hair like sun rays flaring wildly from my bun. The heat rising from the parking lot touched my forehead and made the burn there scream.

Buddy leaned against the trunk of my Pinto, hat in hand, boots crossed at the ankles, as if he had front-row seats at a rodeo and not at the unlucky arena of my life. Behind him, the hood was up. "Had a look," he said, and I felt as though he'd been riffling through my drawers.

The way he stared, squinting, as I walked toward him unnerved me. Then I realized he was looking at my forehead. "Who hit you?" he asked, standing up suddenly and frowning. His fists were clenched, as if he were getting ready for a fight.

"Nobody. Forget it," I said, covering my brow with my hand. "What did you find?"

Buddy put his hat back on, twisted it into the groove of sweaty hair at his crown. "You've been dragging around with a broken alternator belt," he accused.

"I have not," I said.

"Well, your battery's drained dry," he said. "Mom's working on it now."

"Thank God," I said.

"No, thank me," Shelly said as she emerged from

behind the lifted hood. Her ruffled blouse and fingers were smeared with black grease, while her son's hands and clothes were conspicuously clean.

"Thanks, Shelly." I kept myself from kissing her only because Buddy might believe he had one coming.

"I can fix your alternator," Shelly said, "but it'll take more time than you have. Buddy-boy," she asked, trying to sound innocent, "would you mind running Jaime to her job across town?"

I had no choice but to dress in the car.

"Close your eyes," I told Buddy at a stoplight while I pulled on my skirt for The Phoenix underneath the Liberty Bell I was wearing. He obeyed, leaning back against the headrest and puckering his lips as though expecting a kiss.

"Very funny," I said, but I watched him to make sure he didn't peek as I ducked and wriggled out of my Betsy Ross blouse. Buddy waved his arms in front of him like a blind man feeling his way. When he stumbled into the imaginary curtain I'd drawn around myself, I stopped him with a slap.

"Ouch!" he said, kissing his fingers.

"Stay over there," I warned.

Okay, I checked him out. My high school was full of cowboy wannabes in 501s and boots, but Buddy's version of the costume had the look of authenticity. His shirt was creaseless rayon, the sleeves rolled evenly up his sunburned arms. His jeans were unfaded and cut way too tight, secured with a belt buckled with a hood ornament. His boots creaked with newness and pointed, like his collar, at an angle of forty-five degrees. I'd seen this style at the Phoenix airport, on sun-wrinkled farmers who'd come in from their fields to fetch family from California or Idaho. This was the real-life version of Ralph Lauren, what people at my high school called "haute hayseed." But Buddy was no farmer's kid. I could tell that by glancing at his uncalloused hands on the steering wheel.

"Light's green," I told him. "You can open your eyes. Turn here."

"Open?" asked Buddy, blindly swerving onto Camelback. "Did you say open?"

"Buddy!"

"I'm fooling," he said, straightening the car in the lane. "Can't you take a joke?"

"Not today I can't."

True, he ran yellows and his foot was heavy on the gas, but I didn't complain. Whatever got me fast to The Phoenix was all right by me.

While Buddy changed lanes like a racecar driver, I called out directions and tugged at my skirt. I was trying to take it off discreetly, one inch at a time. Though I was careful to keep covered with The Phoenix's uniform, the effort of undressing was embarrassing. Buddy kept his eyes on the road or shut them when I asked him to, but he listened too keenly for the snap of elastic, the metallic rip of a zipper.

"At the rate you're going, you'll still be stripping in the parking lot," he said, when I'd finally gotten the skirt off.

"I'm not stripping, I'm changing!" I yelled, whipping him with the Liberty Bell.

"What's the difference?"

"I knew I should have sat in the back."

"I didn't mean anything by it." Buddy reached over to redirect the air vent, his kind of apology. Cool air rippled my shirt, and temporarily restored my gratitude. He'd get me to The Phoenix, I reminded myself, and on time.

Then, when I flipped down the sun visor to use the mirror, a condom slid out from its hiding place and fell into my lap like a door prize, or like proof. We both looked at the small foil package and then looked away, as if neither of us had the slightest idea or interest in what the thing was.

"Whoa," said Buddy finally. He reached over to grab it, but stopped himself and turned on the stereo instead. The singer pleaded, "Have a little faith in me," and Buddy said, "I guess it's been a few since—"

"Since you've had a girl in this car?" I interrupted. "I hope I haven't taken someone else's scheduled slot!"

"Since anybody's used that mirror, I mean," said

Buddy, breaking out in a blush from his neck to his cheeks.

"Right," I said, opening the glove compartment. "I'll put it in here. It'll be easier to reach."

While Buddy drove in silence, I went back to dressing for work. I put on lipstick hurriedly and brushed out my hair in quick strokes. When I'd finished restyling, I had twisted my hair so tightly my eyebrows were lifted and my head hurt for the rest of the night.

"You'd better pull over," I said when Buddy peeked at me out of the corner of his eye. "Driving's interfering with your view."

"What is it with you, Jaime?" he said, pouting. "You don't even know me, but you act like I'm some dog."

"Your reputation precedes you," I said, surprised at my words—not the teasing, but the barb.

"What did you hear about me?"

"Just the main plot," I said. "The rest I surmised."

Buddy took his hat off then and Frisbeed it to the backseat. He raked his hair with his fingers, sweat smoothing it into glistening ribbons. "Folks change," he said.

"I've heard that."

All right, I'm a sucker for a guy who needs forgiving. But Buddy looked so good there pouting, working his jaw as if he were chewing on a weed, that I suspected the expression had been practiced for a girl or two before me. He reminded me of Dad, who'd

My Life *as a girl*

rehearsed his sorry look so well that when he was arrested, real sorrow settled into his worn-in face.

At a stoplight, Buddy shifted to neutral. The engine sat down, heaving a giant sigh. "What did Casey tell you to make you scared of me?" he asked.

"Scared? I'm not scared," I said, sitting up. But then he turned to me, and I was. Heart pounding, palms sweating, the whole fight-or-flight thing. When he casually reached over and touched the burn-welt on my forehead, I thought my heart would hammer him.

"Is that so?" Buddy said, leaning closer, so close I smelled chlorine. He'd been swimming, I guessed, and the scent made me swoon. Not for Buddy necessarily, but for my old life: our pretty yard with its swimming pool, its warm patio—the time before I knew. *You're staying in Phoenix,* I heard Rosa warning me, *and drowning in a cowboy's blue-green eyes.* I closed my eyes to save myself.

"If you're not afraid of me, then prove it," he said, and I could feel his breath on my mouth, the warning of a kiss. "I dare you to go out dancing with me."

The word *dare* brought me back. My eyes flew open, and my crossed arms came between us like an inflatable life jacket. "I don't have to prove anything," I said, turning away from him to stare out the window. "Especially not to you."

The next mile in the car took forever. Buddy mumbled to the radio, and I untied and tied again the decorative bow on my shoes. When we'd covered enough blacktop to pretend what had happened hadn't, I said, "Next left, just up here."

Buddy asked, "Where's this place we're headed, anyway?"

"You know The Phoenix?"

"Butt-ugly hotel?"

"I work in the restaurant. It's quite elegant."

"Partied there once with some people from El Paso," he said, scowling. "Not my kind of scene." Well, that was one thing Buddy and Rosa would agree on.

Buddy turned into the driveway without signaling, accelerating on the curve. We were speeding toward The Phoenix, past signs posting the twenty-mile-an-hour limit he ignored. Golfers in bright Bermuda shorts flashed by us: green, yellow, red.

"Buddy, slow!" I yelled. "We're here!"

We lurched around the corner. The hotel loomed Aztecesque. As the Mustang slowed at the curb, the hotel doorman took quiet notice. He stood stock-still, but his eyes cased us (as he suspected) casing the joint. When I smiled at him, he looked away.

"Do you dance?" Buddy asked, waving away my offer of a few bucks for gas.

"Dance?" I asked impatiently, cash in one hand, the other on the door. I should leave now, I thought, call out thanks and get out. But something kept me there with Buddy, listening to him rattle on like rolling dice.

My
Life

as a

girl

"Ever been to Boots?" he asked. "Tonight is Ladies' Night."

"I guess you'll have to find some ladies, then," I said, tossing three dollars on the dash.

"Shi-oot, Jaime," said Buddy, opening his door.

"Where are you going?" I asked. I tried my door handle, but it wouldn't budge.

"Sorry—that's broken," Buddy said. He came around and opened my door from outside. "Can't you answer a question without making a joke?" he said, offering his hand.

I hesitated before taking it, but my skirt was as snug as a straightjacket; I couldn't get out of his low-rider car without help. I gripped his fingers (they were surprisingly soft), heaved, and stumbled out to the curb.

He looked hurt for a moment, but then he said, "Madam," so it sounded not classy but cheap. I had to laugh, though, because I did look like a streetwalker: vacuum-packed into my uniform, taking mincing steps toward the employee door. The skirt was designed for restriction of movement, to enforce the speed limit set by the restaurant's piped-in classical music. Or maybe, like at Franklin's, to keep us in our places.

"How about tomorrow?" asked Buddy.

"I'm on at Franklin's."

"Okay, after."

"I'm on at The Phoenix."

"You've gotta take a break sometime," he persisted. "Come on, Jaime."

"Can't you take no for an answer?" I asked.

The doorman raised his eyebrows, as if he wanted to know, too. "He's leaving," I promised, and as if to underline it, I turned back and called out "Bye." But Buddy was still leaning against the Mustang, watching me, tapping the curb with his boot. A loop of his hair had sprung forward, the way it looked in Shelly's photo. I found this weirdly appealing, and far more believable than his mother's hard sell. I bet he's not as bad as he acts, I thought.

Looking back on it now, I'm embarrassed to say that my opinion of Buddy was altered—and my fate that summer changed—by a wayward loop of hair. So it wasn't styled that way, I told myself as I flew into The Phoenix to start my second shift. It sometimes just got loose.

chapter

eight

All that summer, I went to sleep and rose in the morning with the rhythms of waitressing still in my limbs: the tango of The Phoenix, quick steps restrained by that chicly tight skirt; at Franklin's, the breathless trot-trot-trot bump, waltzing in and out of the swinging kitchen door. I don't think anything I've learned in school has gotten into my system so completely as those dining room dances, or the physical memory of hot plates balanced on my forearms, coffee mugs scalding my palms, lifting a loaded dinner tray over my head. I was dead tired every evening, which was all right by me. Waiting tables left me little strength to think about Dad's trial coming up in November, and little time to get into more trouble than he had already caused.

But at Franklin's the next day, trouble arrived with a capital *B*.

Casey and I were cleaning up our stations after the lunch rush, listening to the country station, when Buddy bothered the bells on the restaurant's front door. Casey took one look at him and huffed off to the kitchen. She took the music with her, kicking the door open just as the singer wailed, "I married her just because she looks like you."

Buddy watched her go, shrugging off whatever had been—still was?—between them. Then he took off his hat, fanned his face a few times, and turned to study me. "Did you miss me?" he asked.

"Miss you? I don't even know you," I said, busily cleaning my tables.

"Sure you do," Buddy said, plucking a napkin from a table dispenser to mop his sweaty face. He slumped down into the booth next to the one I was cleaning, stretching both legs out on the seat. His boots, black with red flame stitching, had smooth, spotless soles. "I'm the guy you dreamed about last night," he said.

"You don't know what I—" I began, but then figured I'd better not wrangle with him. "Forget it." His chin was slightly pointed, I noticed, and downy with blond whiskers, which gave him a cute, crafty look, like a chipmunk. Still, there was something about him: his unruly hair maybe, or the strange blue-green color of his eyes.

"Jaime, Jaime, Jaime," he said. He took my hand as I tried to pass by, and palmed instead the soggy, smelly washcloth. "Yech," he said, making a face. He dropped the wet cloth on the table and swirled it around a few times. "There," he said, wiping his hand on his jeans. "All clean. *Now* can you take a break?"

"Buddy!" I said, hating the high-pitched way I sounded, just like a girl.

As I stood there, he plucked another paper napkin from the dispenser, quickly folded it and tore it and twisted it into a swan. I watched as he kept styling napkins, until he'd set out a partner and two baby birds. "For you," he said, lifting the mama bird and landing her in my palm. I couldn't help but laugh at the crude figure, its question-mark neck leaning weakly to one side. "Where did you learn to do that?" I asked.

"Sitting in a diner, working up the nerve to ask you to dance," he said.

"Nerve isn't exactly your weak point," I said, but I could feel that I was blushing. I set the swan down quickly, nudging it across the table toward its mate. "Excuse me," I said, and I reached over to jam a handful of new napkins into the dispenser to replace the ones he'd used. "I've got to get these tables done."

Casey came back through the kitchen door, clutching two clinking bouquets of forks, spoons, and knives. She dropped them noisily onto one of her tables, then stomped back to the kitchen, returning with a rack of clean water glasses. These she slammed onto the bus stand so hard I thought for sure they'd shatter. I noticed she'd loosened her hair from the grimy scrunchy she usually wore, and had reapplied her lipstick, a clown-red shade that shrieked, "Kiss me!"

"You must be here to say you're sorry," Casey said to Buddy, though she spoke to the pile of utensils she pretended to arrange. I followed her, filling napkins.

As far as Casey was concerned, though, she and
Buddy were alone in the room.

"Yeah," said Buddy, looking clueless. "About
that."

"I'm too busy to be kept waiting," said Casey,
a line straight out of the how-to book that was her
bible, *Love Rules*. From the passages she'd quoted to
me so far, you'd think that love had impossible odds.
The book had one chapter on finding a good guy, and
twenty-three chapters on dealing with jerks.

"Casey, I'm—" Buddy started, but she stopped him
midsentence, dramatically raising a fork-filled fist.
"Don't even say it," she commanded. "You know, when
you bailed on me, I went out with Jay." Probably a
white lie, I thought. Despite the *Rules'* claim to help
women "negotiate modern relationships," the book was
just old-fashioned advice for playing hard to get.

"Whatever," said Buddy under his breath.

I tossed the rest of the napkins on the counter in
the waitress station and went to unload the clean water
glasses from the rack. They were still scalding hot from
the dishwasher, so I had to pluck them up with pincher
fingers, using a napkin as a sort of oven mitt.

"Where were you, anyway, not that I care?" asked
Casey, making sure not to look at him while she waited
for his defense.

Buddy looked up at me through his lashes like a
naughty little kid. I could hear his fingers tapping,
running in circles as if chasing something, on the vinyl

booth seat. "I had an emergency," he said, and it occurred to me he meant the ride he'd given me yesterday. I realized then that *I* was the reason Buddy hadn't kept their date.

"An emergency," Casey echoed. The words smoldered in her throat, turning her neck red, then her face. I'd seen her scream at grouchy Estevez for messing up an order, so I didn't want to know what she'd say if she thought I had messed with her love life. "What kind of emergency?" she asked, and I swear I saw smoke begin to spiral out of her ears.

"Jaime..." Buddy began, and for a perilous moment, he turned and looked at me. I just kept on stacking hot glasses as carefully as if they were crystal, but I wanted to scream from the suspense.

"Jaime?" said Casey, as if my name were crazy. "What does Jaime have to do with you not showing up? Not that it was a big deal, not that I didn't have other plans."

Plans? I thought, I'll show you plans—and they all begin with leaving the state. I often had the same dream in which I glimpsed someone familiar in a crowd, then lost her before I could catch up. "Easy dream," Rosa told me. "That person is yourself." But finding her wasn't so easy; an entire country lay between who I was and who I wanted to be. The weird thing was, I *had* dreamed of Buddy the night before, just as he'd said. We were in his car at a stoplight. He leaned against the headrest, eyes closed, waiting for my kiss.

"Ouch!" I cried as a glass slipped to the faux-brick floor and shattered, throwing shards against my feet. I bent down to clean up the mess.

"I'll get it," said Casey, suddenly Miss Cooperative, though normally she couldn't be bothered to water your tables on her way by. Crouching beside me, she leaned in close and whispered, "Go on back to the kitchen, would you, so Buddy and I can talk."

"Sure," I said, rising quickly to lift the empty rack. "If you can talk and set my tables at the same time." I felt like a kid being sent to her room, the way I'd always been sent when my parents had a fight.

I left Casey and Buddy to each other, sure they'd be a couple again by the end of the shift. In the kitchen, I poured myself a glass of water and sat down at the lunch table to count my tip money, mostly change but also a handful of bills. This gave me the same sneaky pleasure I used to feel checking out the forty shades of eye shadow I'd collected from the Palo Verde Pharmacy. When Mom and Dad were screaming at each other, I'd line up the colors on my dresser, from Peachy Keen to Kohl. I spent an hour sometimes re-arranging them, pastels and primaries, or in rainbow order, ROYGBIV.

"Good day?" asked Kenny, coming out of his office and sitting down in the chair opposite.

"Pretty good," I said, stuffing the money back into my vinyl tip pouch. I preferred to count my Future in secret, enjoyed the ritual of stacking the quarters, "facing" the bills. Just the prospect of counting my tips could cheer me when customers spoke to me rudely or kept me at their tables chatting while my orders petrified under the warming lamps. Some days, money was my sole motivation for dragging myself out of bed. I often found myself looking past the actual people sitting at my tables, seeing in their places three bucks or five or seven.

"Good, good," said Kenny, wiping the sweat from my water glass with his pointer finger. Our real conversations often went on beneath the surface, while we exchanged no more than a few audible words. Ten words was our record, a conversation in which we'd established that I'd be nice to Kenny if he'd keep his hands to himself. "Tables done?" he asked.

Five, I thought, counting words instead of coins now. "Almost," I said. *Six.*

"Keep up the good work." A record-breaking exchange. Kenny smiled and skulked back into his office, and I resumed counting my spoils.

Between three and four on weekdays, the diner was usually dead. Estevez and the Hobart had retreated to the parking lot to smoke cigarettes, adding to a castle of crushed butts by the back door. (I never did learn the Hobart's real name—people called him by the brand name of the dishwashing machine he operated.) Mark, the prep cook, was cleaning his station, his buzzed hair held back with a red bandanna. He had studied engineering at the University of Iowa, then had come west looking for work. I wondered if, after six years of sunning and buffing at Gold's Gym, he'd begun to call himself a cook.

When he'd finished, he took off his apron and flung it to the floor. Though Mark was fastidious about his appearance, everywhere he went he left a messy trail behind. "Where's your cohort?" he asked, meaning Casey, for whom he harbored a wicked crush. He admired her because she had the guts to take on Estevez. I just thought she was mean.

"She's making up with her boyfriend," I said.

"That Buddy guy? I thought he was here for you."

"He's not my type," I said, as if I'd had enough experience to have a type, like those compact blondes from my high school, who came shrink-wrapped with the guys in the *Risky Business* shades.

Mark came around the counter, tucking his shirt into his jeans. "Can't he take her someplace nicer than Franklin's?" he asked me. "I'd take her to The Phoenix for a drink by the pool."

"Funny you should mention The Phoenix," I said, glancing at the wall clock. I zipped up my tip pouch and slid it back into my apron. It was time to step back onto the treadmill of my endless double shift.

Just then Casey came through the door, looking flushed and defeated.

"The Coyote is having a twofer on melon margaritas," Mark offered.

"I could use one," Casey said, grabbing her bag. Mark could hardly believe his good fortune. He backed out of the doorway, his fingers raised over her head in a victory sign. I gathered my things and left the way I usually did, out the front.

Buddy caught my hand as I entered the dining room, and twirled me so we were standing side by side. "Shift's over," he said, as if I needed to be reminded. "*Now* will you dance?" His arm snaked in around my waist and settled dangerously on the small of my back. "Watch my feet," he said, hop-stepping forward. "This is called the Texas two-step."

"I can't do this," I said, trying to extricate myself. "I can't even keep a beat." The truth was, I couldn't keep someone else's; I hadn't danced with a boy since fifth grade, when I'd learned to square-dance at Camp Buffalo Roam.

"Just follow."

"I can't."

"Then lead."

"Very funny." I looked over his shoulder for Casey, but she was nowhere in sight. "Buddy, I can't do this!" I pleaded.

"Jaime," said Buddy, so close to my ear I got goose bumps. "You *are*."

I stopped fighting then and followed, watching Buddy's boots slide and kick across the floor. He had a nice way of ignoring my blunders, the too many times I stepped on his toes. He just kept on moving—moving me—smoothly, his hand lightly resting on my back. His body beside mine felt solid and sure.

"You're good at this," I said as we traversed the dining room, stepping across the colonial brick floor. "You make the missteps seem part of it."

Gently urging me around, he said, "I know what it's like to screw up royally."

"So I'm not the only spaz."

"I don't mean dancing. I mean drinking too much, fighting in bars."

"Oh," I said. "You don't do those things anymore?"

"Not since I met you," he said, stopping so suddenly I crashed into him. He reached out to steady me, and I wondered how much of the sick, jumpy feeling people like to call love was just the excitement of being cornered, the certainty of being caught. Buddy whispered, "When I want to, I can be really good."

"Buddy," I said, looking down at my feet as we began to dance again. I didn't want to look at him, for fear that I would smile. I was afraid that having fun made me guilty by association, turned me back into that no-good con man's girl. But as we began to dance again, laughter rushed from my throat like a confession. Soon I was laughing so hard I was helpless, swaying in Buddy's arms.

Buddy did his best to support me. "What's so funny?" he asked.

"This! Us!" I said, as I twirled away from him. The room spun, and I orbited, tethered to his hand. I felt dizzy and reckless, as if he'd cast me out and reeled back the old lucky Jaime who wasn't afraid to gamble.

Of course, that's when Kenny burst through the kitchen door, two-fisted with ketchups. "Buddy," he said, trying to look surprised.

Buddy just nodded in his direction, then said loudly enough for Kenny's ears, "Let me take you out tonight, show you some more steps."

"I'm working past midnight."

"Midnight, then," he said. Despite his surefooted moves he was trembling, and when he spoke his cheek twitched nervously. "Later," he said to Kenny, then turned and ducked out the door, flipping Franklin's OPEN sign to CLOSED.

"That guy's a menace," said Kenny. "If I were you, I wouldn't trust him."

"We were just goofing," I said.

The truth was, I trusted Buddy, the way I believed in my birthday lottery number, rabbits' feet, lucky dice. I told myself the *real* Buddy was beneath all the bravado, that he was as hurt and hopeful as I was.

chapter

nine

It was nearly midnight when I got home from my shift at The Phoenix. Mom was asleep sitting up in the family room, a magazine of crossword puzzles open in her lap. On the TV, an evangelist barked out directions to the Mountain Kingdom Cathedral: "Tatum and Shea Boulevard! Everyone welcome!"

I switched off the set out of habit, and the sudden silence made Mom jerk her head back. "Jaime?" she said. Her hair was crushed on one side, her eyes naked without her glasses. She looked so vulnerable, hardly like the mother I knew or the sturdy girl from her stories of growing up.

Mom had come from a family of fighters—the Wynn women, all of them tall with broad, strong faces and flat cheeks like warriors' shields. Until she married, they'd all lived on the same street in Yuma, Arizona, like a female barricade. Her mother, Mary-Rita, started a cantaloupe farm after her husband left her with orchards of inferior oranges. Her sister Jo Ellen disguised herself as a boy to pitch for the Criminals at Yuma High (formerly the territorial

My Life *as a girl*

prison). Her sister Henri(etta) once stole a meat truck and crashed the Desert Debutante dinner dance 200 miles away in Phoenix. And Johnna, my mother, the undisputed beauty of the family, redeemed herself by standing up to a bad boy named Spider Reid. People said I took after Mom, though I was more like a Cody. I was puny in her presence, a full five inches shorter, and not nearly as pretty at eighteen as she'd been then.

"How was work tonight?" she asked.

"I'm so tired I can't see straight."

"Good night, then," she said sleepily, patting around her seat for the remote.

"Mom?" I paused in the doorway. "Why don't you just go to bed?" It drove me crazy the way she drank coffee in the evenings so she could sit up until all hours fighting sleep. Frowning, flipping channels, she said, "I think there's something good on the late-late." But after I'd washed up and changed out of my uniform, I peeked into the family room and saw she was asleep again.

In my room, I opened the window to air perfumed by chlorine—air that, at midnight, was still one hundred degrees. I stood there for a moment, listening to the soundtrack of my childhood: the shrieking cicadas, the pulse and hum of pool pumps up and down the block. In our old house, I used to sit on the pool deck with my parents as the sun descended over the oleanders like a gaudy New Year's ball. The day's warmth radiated from the stucco as they told stories about meeting and falling in love.

"Your father saved my cat's life after I nearly killed him with the lawn mower," Mom would begin, licking the salt from the rim of her margarita glass. Dad had been employed by her family for the summer. I'd seen pictures of him standing in a field lined by dry irrigation ditches, his hair neatly parted and combed through with grease.

"Nearly killed the cat, that is," Dad always added. "Not your dad."

It was one of my favorite stories—how my father ripped the shirt off his back and used it for a tourniquet to save Mom's poor old cat Useless from bleeding to death.

"The way he wrapped that cat with such confidence!" Mom said. "And held on, even when Useless, blind in one eye and scared to death, scratched trenches into his arm!" Dad would stroke his forearm gingerly, though the skin he touched was unscarred and evenly tanned. "You have to admire a man who'll make that kind of gesture," she said, though Useless probably suffered more with a side full of stitches than he would have had my father just let him be.

In Mom's stories, Dad was always a hero and their marriage destiny. I had already seen enough to know better. But anything seemed possible as we sat there together on our old pool deck, in the slanting light of early evening.

My

Life

as a

girl

*   *   *

I lifted myself over the window sill and landed noisily on the granite gravel. Then, without looking back, I ran past our complex of rented bungalows, heading for an aging eucalyptus at the end of the street.

That's where I'd told Buddy to meet me, the Big Tree, where kids used to fight after school. I'd seen Joey Favata and Laura Foxman go at it once, pounding each other while a crowd of kids watched. Laura's tube top had slipped down to expose her breasts, and Joey, stunned by the sight, let her punch him right in the mouth. One of his front teeth was lost that day, buried somewhere beneath the Big Tree.

Now the hot, heavy air tasted of memory—coconut and orange, sweat and cooling mud—as I scratched the ground with my sandals, almost expecting to unearth Joey's tooth. "Just this once," I'd told Buddy when he'd called The Phoenix to ask if I'd go dancing. *Hurry, Buddy,* I was thinking as I drew circles in the dirt. *Before I change my mind.*

Boots was in the old part of town, next to an abandoned department store. Buddy double-parked behind an emerald green Monte Carlo, a gang car Rosa called a sex mobile. In the parking lot, he took my hand without permission and pulled open the wide oak door.

The music was loud and I was grateful. The ride to the club had been excruciating, mostly silence punctuated with the question *What am I doing?* slamming back and forth in my brain. Now we held hands easily as we stood at the corral fence that penned in the dancers on the raised platform floor. The men all looked like Buddy, in Stetsons and tight jeans and big-buckled belts. The women wore too much makeup and blouses with silky fringe that slapped their chests when they twirled. I watched a woman in black jeans and gray snakeskin boots spin and kick and promenade with one man after another. She was too skinny, I thought, and there was nothing special about her face. But she was a joyful, graceful dancer, who made her partners look good.

"Want a drink?" asked Buddy. I turned to answer, and he placed his hat on my head. The hat teetered loosely; it was warm around the band. I nodded and followed him to the bar, knowing words would be lost in the noise and rhythmic stamping of feet. I had decided, though I hadn't actually said the words to myself, that I would drink whatever he ordered for me.

"Rum and Coke?" the bartender yelled.

"A virgin for her," said Buddy, tipping the hat forward, so that I was briefly blinded. "And a Coors for me." We set these on the corral fence as the music turned slow and weepy. Buddy reclaimed his hat, then took my hand again and led me out to the floor.

At high school dances, slow songs were an invitation to grope and stumble with the cool boys, who hung out on the sidelines, waiting to be asked. But here, partners held hands and stepped together. Men clearly knew their parts. As we walked out to join them,

Buddy's boots clicked neatly on the floor, and mine slap-thudded in my Birkenstocks.

"Rattlesnake," he whispered.

"I don't know it," I said.

"I'll teach you," he said, slipping his arm around my waist.

The Rattlesnake was a variation on a waltz, a sweeping turn step. Partners spun in an S across the floor, then back in the opposite direction. Half the dance I was leading, half the time following backward. Moving forward, I always stumbled, my mind moving faster than my feet. "Close your eyes," Buddy said, his words buzzing in my ear. "Don't think. Just go." I did, and I still stumbled, though it was easier with my eyes closed to imagine moving with grace. Buddy turned me, and we made our way back down the floor and up again.

We were both winded when we finished, holding hands sticky with sweat.

"Let's get a booth," said Buddy.

"I'll meet you," I said, still a bit dizzy. "I'm going to the little cowgirls' room."

In the bathroom, the stalls were big enough to keep horses, paneled with Formica in a spicy barn red. In one of them, I heard a woman quietly weeping. In another, a voice said, "Blow him out of your system, honey," while another woman retched.

At the mirror, troweling mascara, was a girl from my eighth-grade softball team. Before a game once, she'd gone off with an umpire who must have been thirty. I remembered how she'd missed warmups, and how she couldn't hit when she finally did come back. Though she'd terrified me back then, bragging about what she'd done with whom, now I found myself saying boldly, "Caitlin? Caitlin McCourt?"

Caitlin turned a glum face pale with powder, bucking the trend in Arizona of tanning to burn. Maybe to make up for her Etch-a-Sketch eyebrows, her hair was hot-rollered into a national monument and glue-gunned into place. "That's me," she said.

"Jaime Cody," I said. "The Quails? I played third base?"

Caitlin picked up a pack of cigarettes and a kachina doll lighter. She had the butane set as high as it would go, so when she cracked back the little doll's head, a wall of fire leaped out, hot and high enough to burn a hole right through her brain. She took a long drag on her cigarette, then snapped the lighter closed with her thumb.

"You hung with that chick Rosa," she said finally. "She was cool. What's up with her?"

"She's around," I said, regretting I hadn't introduced myself as the over-the-fence home run champ. "I'm not here with Rosa, though," I told her. "I'm here with Buddy Holt."

"Buddy Holt?" she said, taking in my straight hair, T-shirt, boy's jeans. I enjoyed her surprise and the flattery of her second look. But then she turned back to the mirror and began blackening her lashes. "Don't know him," she said. "But say hi to Rosa."

"I will," I said, fourteen again, Rosa's side-kick, as the bathroom door swung closed behind me.

Buddy called me over to a booth he shared with another couple, a girl named Diane and a grim-looking guy he introduced as his cousin Jim. "You guys looked great out there," said Diane. "I sure wish I could dance." She knocked the plastic plate of her hip brace, a souvenir from her recent trip through the window of Jim's Jeep.

"Ran into a cactus," Jim explained, shrugging, as if it happened every day.

"At least it keeps me from eating," Diane said, digging into her purse. "I'll be way skinny by the time it comes off."

"And I'll be ready to jump your bones," said Jim. Diane laughed and took out a cosmetic mirror backed with inlaid abalone, tapping it against a vial of white powder.

I'd seen cocaine before, in the bathroom at my high school, passed around in plain sight at the graduation party. Rosa and I didn't do drugs. Rosa would give you her reasons in a complicated speech about political oppression and personal accountability. My reason was simpler: terror of losing control.

Buddy frowned at her. "Uncool," he said, nodding in my direction.

Jim said, "Put it away."

Diane dropped the vial into her bag and took out a

lipstick, as if she'd only picked the wrong tube.

"What do you think, Jim?" asked Buddy. "Did I hook up with a babe or what?" That unnerved me more than the cocaine, so much that I nearly spit out my drink. I knew the difference between pretty and sexy. The word *babe* had last been used to describe me back before I learned to walk.

"Jaime's a nice girl," said Jim, rolling his beer cap between his thumb and finger.

Diane leaned over the table, saying, "We should all try to be a bit nicer." She was the real babe, her voice warm with powder-stoked love.

Jim nodded without conviction as the dance track ended and the house band, Grand Rio, swarmed the stage.

The lead singer, Tom Rio, was dressed in black, with a studded belt, like you'd see on a cartoon bulldog, roped around his thick waist. He adjusted his guitar against his belly. "Hello, Phoenix!" he yelled, as if Boots were just one of many stops on an exciting journey. Before he began playing, he picked up a bottle of whiskey that had been left on one of the speakers, prompting the audience to give an appreciative roar. His hands were trembling as he held up the bottle like a trophy, yelling, "Let's get loaded!"

The band played so loudly I could barely hear the melody beneath the pounding drums, so loudly we were stunned into our seats. Occasionally, Buddy would lean into me and shout above the band, "Isn't this great?" The music was painful to listen to, but it did relieve us of the awkward obligation to speak.

Then I laid my arm on the table, and Buddy stretched his out alongside mine. He'd cuffed his shirt to his elbow, and the coarse hair on his arms made mine stand on end. I moved my arm away a bit, to see if he would follow.

He did.

My fists unclenched, my fingers stretched and stroked the waxy table. Buddy moved closer. I didn't even hear the music, I was so focused on the place where our arms touched each other, the warm, tingling strip of skin. In my mind, I brushed his lips with my fingers, gathered the hair at the nape of his neck. It was like stealing; I didn't even look at him. Anyone who saw me saw a girl who looked slightly bored and out of place, just listening to the band.

The sun was already rising by the time Buddy dropped me off. "Stop here," I told him a half-block from our apartment, and he pulled over to the curb. I was trying to think of a line from a movie, something witty and casual, when Buddy leaned across my seat and finally kissed me.

His skin smelled like smoke and beer, scents that used to mean Dad was home late, empty-pocketed, and there was going to be a fight. The scent was both familiar and mysterious. I knew it; I wanted to know more.

"Jaime," he whispered, "I want to…"

"You want to what?"

He took my hand and kissed it. "I want to start out right with you." He eased me down onto the car seat, slipping a hand under my shirt. I breathed in sharply, and he quickly withdrew it, moving it to rest on my shoulder. "I'm sorry," he whispered. "I was just trying to touch your heart."

I laughed and reached for his hand, placing it just above my left breast. "Here," I said, feeling my heart beat against his fingers. "If you want to touch my heart—here."

"It's running all right," he said, grinning. He ducked his head to listen. "In fact, it's beating pretty hard."

"It hasn't quit dancing yet," I said. I gave in to the urge to comb his hair through my fingers, the gesture stirring ghosts of boys I'd loved, or thought I had.

"I like that," Buddy said. Probably he wasn't thinking of me either, but of some idea of a girlfriend. He squinted as though he were trying to make the picture come clearer. Then suddenly he said, "Jaime, can I ask you something?"

"Ask me," I said. I expected the sex question; every boyfriend asked it sooner or later with his venturing hands.

"Would you go with me to church?"

I'd been leaning back against the seat where he'd placed me, but I pulled myself upright and folded my hands primly in my lap. "Church?" I said.

Buddy glanced at the car clock. "It starts at

My
Life

as a

girl

eleven," he said. "How about if I come by at ten?"

"All right," I said. I was charmed, but also wary; I felt as if I'd signed on to something important without first reading the fine print. Buddy twisted toward me, pulling his legs underneath him so he was sitting on his knees. "I'll be so good with you, Jaime," he whispered between kisses, holding my face as if his hands and arms were a pedestal. "Just let me try."

No boy before had ever spoken to me so earnestly; it was like being offered the secret handshake that allowed me entry to the BOYS ONLY fort. I wasn't so naive that I believed him, though I really wanted to. Whatever deal we'd struck for Buddy to be good, I think I knew even then that I was betting on him to be bad.

"Ten, then," I said, pulling away finally and climbing out of the car. Buddy drove alongside slowly until I waved him off.

I walked back to our apartment, surprised by how new and hopeful our neighborhood looked in the morning just before the sun rose. I felt awake and courageous as I crawled back in through my bedroom window, as if I were the world's guardian.

At ten twenty, Buddy picked me up in new clothes and a new-looking Lexus the color of money. Mom took in the car and his Stetson. "Which church?" she quizzed me as Buddy idled in the driveway. "What time is the service over? Where did you meet this boy?"

"Mom," I whined, "I'm just going to *church*."

She stood at the front door scowling as I climbed into Buddy's car. "Don't forget your shift at The Phoenix," she called out as I closed the door.

"This isn't Shelly's car, is it?" I said to Buddy, rubbing my palms on the powder-soft seats.

"Bought it this morning," he said, raising his eyebrows in the rearview. "I wanted something classy to drive you to church."

"I *like* your Mustang," I blurted.

"Really?" Buddy asked. "Then I'll just junk this car." He lurched out of the driveway. "Buddy!" I grabbed the armrest and held on.

"I'm just kidding."

"About buying it or taking it back?"

"Both. You met my cousin Jim last night? He's a mechanic. After he works on a car, I test-drive it around town to make sure it's running all right." As usual, the truth was less interesting than the story. "Oh," I said, stifling a yawn.

Rising alongside rows of spindly date palms was the white steeple of the Desert Baptist, an angular, neutered construction designed by Frank Lloyd Wright. The steeple's shadow fell across the open courtyard, and Buddy and I watched as clean-looking families crossed over it and entered through the pale oak doors. Then, just as the funereal music began, we slipped inside and found an empty pew.

My Life as a girl

I stood there like an impostor, songbook in hand, reading one verse ahead so that I could appear confident while singing a hymn I barely knew. The vast ceiling, trembling organ music, and warped soprano choir made me want to holler, the way I used to want to muddy my Grandma Cody's white carpet when she made us leave our shoes at the door.

My own family wasn't the kind you'd call "church-going," though I'd tried on religion a few times. I'll admit that my actual knowledge of the Scriptures, a handful of holiday stories, was odd and spotty, like a view of the world pieced together by reading photo captions in *National Geographic*. Buddy's religious training seemed even more shaky. He was out of tune on "Glory, Glory," and his lips moved mutely during the Lord's Prayer. Still, when I peeked at him through my lashes, his eyes were open, trained on the stained-glass Crucifixion, his expression one of genuine awe.

"It gets better," Buddy whispered when the prayer was over. "This preacher's pretty wild." He took my hand as the minister motioned for the congregation to sit down.

Without the proper moral pruning, my idea of God had grown and twisted into something both ineffable and cartoonish: the character on the Cracker Jack box, a stylized WWII navy man with flowing, bell-bottomed white pants. This image of the Cracker Jack God confirmed me, comforting, much like the childish prayer I'd begun saying when all the trouble started with Dad.

"Why God's Word Matters" was the title of the sermon advertised on the electric sign outside. But Reverend Wilcox didn't start with a top-ten list of answers. He began instead by asking a question: "Who here today is in love?"

Benches squeaked as the congregation shifted, unsure how to answer—verbally? a show of hands?—too shy to reveal something so personal right there in God's house. But suddenly, there was Buddy, unabashedly waving his arms like some guy out in center field coaxing a fly ball from the air.

"Young man, is that a yes?" asked Reverend Wilcox. He laughed, and added good-naturedly, "I'll pause for a moment while you all turn around to see the young woman he's with."

Luckily, the spotlight lasted only briefly, until I'd sunk as far down as I could into my seat. Then Reverend Wilcox held up a copy of the Bible. "'For now we see in a mirror dimly, but then face to face; now I know in part, but then I shall know full just as I also have been full known. But now abide faith, hope, love, these three; but the greatest of these is love.' Ring a bell, anyone?"

The passage—1 Corinthians: 13—was the only one I'd memorized, having heard it said at countless cousins' weddings. The lines defining love had almost lost their meaning from rote repetition, like the colonial history my grade school teachers retreaded every year just in case we hadn't understood the lesson the first five or six times. But Reverend Wilcox put a talk show spin on the topic, walking out into the congregation and brandishing copies of glossy magazines.

"Here's one that promises to tell you how to bond with your baby," he said, dangling the magazine in front of a woman holding a newborn. "And here," he said, flinging a magazine to a man seated across the aisle. "This one guarantees it'll help you get along with your boss." The audience tittered as he motioned to the "boss" sitting next to him, presumably the man's wife.

He jogged to the back of the church then, making a beeline toward Buddy and me. "Here's one that lets you in on the secrets of a man's heart," he said, dangling a copy of *Cosmo* in front of us. I saw that his eyes were merry, not malicious. He paused and fanned through the pages theatrically. "Oh, boy," he said, rolling his eyes and folding the magazine shut. "This one I'd better not distribute." Softly, for our benefit only, he said, "Be careful with each other. The heart is where the soul resides."

Then he turned and bounded back up the aisle to his pulpit. "We spend millions every year on these magazines," he said, tossing the pile in his arms to the floor. "Because we have questions about whom we should love, how we should live our lives. We read these articles as if our very lives depended upon it. Well, I'm here to tell you about a more reliable source, the ultimate expert." He picked up the Bible and let it fall again heavily—*thump!*—to his reading stand.

"Take a tip from God," he said, flipping pages. "'Love is patient. Love is kind.'"

The mood in the congregation lightened, as people slowly realized their relationships would be spoken of generally and not, as they'd feared, put to trial. I laid my hand over my heart, imagining what my soul would look like as I pondered Reverend Wilcox's words. Buddy leaned forward and squeezed my thigh, whispering, "I told you he was wild."

Afterward, in the Lexus, Buddy kissed me, touching my face, my neck, my shoulders urgently, as if reassuring himself of my presence over and over again. His expression was reverent and unguarded, which only strengthened my desire to take care of him. I was thinking how inside each of us was a mystery: an angel in an airy temple, a flame burning inside a bone lantern, a nervous rodent chewing on the bars of a bamboo cage. Real love required a leap of faith past appearances, didn't it? "Be careful with each other," the minister had said.

"Buddy, slow down," I said, as he pressed against me, dangerously close to what I had just realized was my fragile heart.

"I know," he groaned. "'Love is patient.'"

I placed his hands on the steering wheel. "Among other things," I said. "Drive."

I knew that Buddy would have to meet my mother if I wanted to see him again. "That's cool," he said, adjusting his Stetson in the rearview. "I'm good with moms." But then, Buddy had never had to meet Johnna (formerly Cody) Wynn.

We found her inside folding laundry at the kitchen table, wearing one of her mortifying snap-front, day-off smocks. "How was church?" she asked over her shoulder.

"Holy," said Buddy.

Mom turned sharply around.

"This is Buddy Holt," I said. "You wanted to meet him."

Buddy didn't take off his hat, as boys were supposed to. He raised his hand lazily, a half-mast high-five. "Hey," he said.

"Hello," said Mom, two degrees below lukewarm.

We all stood there for an awkward moment among the piles of warm towels and pajamas and assorted lingerie. What was he supposed to say: Nice smock? Nice bras? Finally, Mom went back to folding laundry, and Buddy pulled out a chair, which screamed against the linoleum. "Okay if I sit?" he asked when Mom glared at him.

"I wasn't going to stop you," she said.

I wanted Mom to see Buddy as I had at church: the lost boy who would flourish given faith, hope, love. But part of me was relieved she saw right through him. She regarded him with appropriate suspicion—suspicion that would have been useful back when Dad was looting my piggy bank.

And Buddy, both hulking and diminished in Mom's

presence, wasn't helping matters any. He swaggered like a bully from one of her old stories. "So ask me," he said, predictably surly. "You want to know what I'm doing with your daughter, right?"

Mom stopped folding. "My understanding was that you were taking Jaime to church." With her eyes, she willed Buddy's elbow off a pile of washcloths and stripped him of his swagger as well. "Yes, ma'am," he said, sitting up straight the way my father did with traffic cops. "That's exactly what we did."

"So I don't need to wonder."

"No, ma'am."

"Good."

That was it. Buddy rose noiselessly. I walked him to his car.

"Your mom's pretty harsh," he said when we were out of earshot. I could tell she'd hurt his feelings. He wouldn't look at me.

"She's just protective," I said. "I'm her only child."

"Usually it's dads you have to look out for."

"My parents are divorced," I lied, to close the subject.

"Yeah," said Buddy. "Me too." Then just as suddenly, he was over it. He grinned and took my hand. "If I were your mom," he said, glancing back at the kitchen window to make sure Mom was watching, "I'd never let you out of my sight." Then he gave me a kiss that could have melted glass.

*   *   *

My
Life

as a

girl

Inside, Mom and I folded laundry without speaking, snapping and cornering a sweet-smelling sheet. "If there's anything I hate," Mom said finally, "it's being called ma'am."

"You could give him a chance."

"He's sneaky, Jaime," she said. "When I was a young woman, living under my parents' roof on our cantaloupe farm, I knew a boy named Spider Reid..."

I groaned. I was grouchy from sleep deprivation and, besides, I hated the gleam in her eye when she talked about Spider, always cast as the bad boy who'd lost out to my virtuous dad.

"Spider was a real smart aleck," she continued as I began stacking underwear, just two piles now, not three. "He took apart his T-Bird once, then reassembled it inside the high school's Home Ec classroom."

"Scandalous," I said. "Did he disrupt the lesson on baking banana bread?" I rolled my eyes, though I'd always liked imagining that red car showing up like a challenge among the pink kitchenettes.

"He was dangerous!" Mom insisted. "And sneaky. The kind of boy who had a tattoo under his shirt sleeve of two bulging, naked breasts."

"Breast envy," I said, looking down at my own heirloom flat chest. "So what did he see in you?"

"Very funny," Mom said. "I was too good for him. Spider had no ambition. Not like your—" She stopped herself short. Dad's ambition had finally taken the form of a felony, and so it was a topic we tried to avoid. While Mom caught her place again, I grabbed my Phoenix uniform from the basket and fanned myself, hoping to cool it before I put it on.

"Can we fast-forward to the moral?" I said. "I've got to get to work."

"Spider was a liar and a big talker," Mom said. "One night he scrawled all over the boys' room door, telling the whole school I slept with him."

"A lie," I said, though I had long suspected otherwise. My parents told their stories in tandem—all except this one. Whenever Mom talked about Spider, Dad jumped to refill drinks, then hovered hostlike on the sidelines.

"So late one night," she continued, "Henri and Jo and I dumped a bushel full of rotten tomatoes into the backseat of his beloved T-Bird." As she talked, I saw the three sisters as if I, too, had been there: clad in their sweet nightgowns, emptying out their baskets and then flying away through the cantaloupe fields. Mom laughed, saying, "I don't imagine Spider got comfortable in that car with any girl after that."

"That would be a pretty sticky affair," I replied, as Dad always did, his jokes protecting him from an old lover's jab.

In nowhere Yuma, such a stunt was newsworthy, though Mom's identity was protected in the paper. Readers were left to draw their own conclusions from the headline: BETRAYED.

My
Life
as a
girl

"Spider married some poor waif straight out of high school," Mom said, shaking her head, "and left her in labor with child number five."

"What a jerk," I said.

"It just goes to show you," said Mom. "Thank the Lord my mother told me I was meant for better things." In the old days, this had been the part where she'd take my father's hand, and all the jagged pieces of our lives would come together. In our family, storytelling was truce-making, a way of proclaiming your willingness to forgive and forget. Now Mom frowned as she looked out the window at the courtyard we shared with other broken families who'd stopped at the Oasis Apartments temporarily. I had to get into my uniform, and so I left her there searching for just the right ending.

chapter

ten

Back-Easters have some weird ideas about the West. "Did you ride a horse to school?" my soon-to-be roommate asked in her first letter. Rosa said she might as well have asked if we were required to wear shoes.

It was true Amanda's inquiries about cowboys and Indians and ranch life showed that what she knew of Arizona was based on cowboy movies filmed at Castle Rock. I didn't fault her for it. I pictured her life like *The Philadelphia Story*, heard her speaking with Katharine Hepburn's accent, as foreign to me as the movie character's stone-mansion wealth.

Every line of Amanda's letters sighed with exhaustion brought on by social obligation: orchestra concerts and poetry readings and a debutante party planned for December. She didn't seem to have or need a summer job. To me, Amanda *was* Bryn Mawr: brilliant, cultured, rich. I still felt like the Admissions mistake.

"'Phoenix is so charming, isn't it?'" Rosa said, quoting from Amanda's latest letter, which I already regretted sharing. "Have you told her you're dating a real-life cowboy?"

"He's not a cowboy, Rosa," I said, digging in my bag for sunglasses. "That's just the way he dresses."

"What's up with that?" said Rosa. "Should I walk around in a white coat because I want to be a doctor?"

"You act like my mother," I teased her, "so maybe that's how you should dress. Besides, we're just dancing."

"Right," Rosa said. "And you'd better get out of Phoenix before you wake up and find yourself walking down the aisle with Buddy, wearing a prairie skirt."

"Married?" I said. "Never." Rosa planned to marry and have kids, but to me, a family was the rock that could derail my train.

It was a Saturday, and we were wasting our day off in the Oasis courtyard, talking and sipping sugary iced coffee. Quartz-speckled concrete surrounded the small island of grass where we'd set up our chairs. We had to keep moving as the sun did across the white-hot, cloudless sky.

"'You know how dads are,'" Rosa read aloud from Amanda's letter, so I knew she'd reached the part about the convertible he'd bought her for her birthday.

"Yep, dads," I said, picturing mine in a prison-issue jumpsuit. Secretly, I was flattered that Amanda assumed our families had anything in common. The last thing I wanted was to set the record straight. And so my letters back were filled with funny stories about waiting tables, as though I were some cultural anthropologist and not just in need of fast cash. I described our old house as if we still lived there. I told her my father still sold insurance, and made my mom the owner of the bakery where she worked. I lied, and called my lies storytelling, just as my parents did.

Rosa folded up the letter. "If you ask me," she said, "this chick is spoiled."

"I wish we could go swimming," I said, to change the subject.

"We could go to the Cactus Center," Rosa said, meaning the city pool, crowded with kids under ten.

"I'm not swimming anywhere they have to remind you not to wee-wee in the water," I said.

"What about The Phoenix?" asked Rosa.

"Sure, if I want to lose my job."

"*¿Cómo no?* You live at that hotel. They won't let you use the pool?"

"Ask Ms. Pickett. Employees aren't allowed." I got up to turn on the lawn sprinklers, using an iron prong that hung on a secret hook behind a row of cypress trees. "Watch it," I said to Rosa. "Don't get that letter wet."

Rosa held the letter at arm's length as the sprinklers rose and sprayed, the tiny horizontal windmills watering our skin. I let them run as long as I dared, all the while keeping watch for the landlord, a gray-faced man who, if he caught me, would probably add July's water bill to our rent.

"Amanda says she's heard it's a dry heat in

Phoenix," said Rosa. "So I guess we shouldn't
worry about it getting to a hundred and twelve."

"Dry like an oven," I said, turning off the
water and settling back into my chaise. "Dry
like swinging open the gates of hell."

"And I hate how she calls her nap *siesta*,"
Rosa added.

"*You* say it," I said, regretting the word I'd
included, for color, in my last letter east.

"Yeah, but she means *lazy*, like those stone boys
with giant sombreros that Anglos put on their lawns.
And here"—she opened the letter again and jabbed it
with her finger—"where she wishes her life were simpler? She's dissing you. She means you come from a
cow town."

"What about Rollergirl?" I said. Rosa's roommate
had sent a picture of herself skating and a letter detail-
ing a fanatical fitness routine. "I'm surprised she
hasn't flown out here from Oregon or wherever and
measured your flab with one of those caliper things."

Rosa grinned. "I'll be so buff by December you
won't recognize me."

"Don't even say that," I said. I intended to come
home from college a new person, but the idea of Rosa
changing filled me with dread.

She swatted me with the letter. "Don't worry, I'll
still hang with you even if you come home in knee
socks and one of those little field hockey skirts."

"No way," I told her. "Actually, I was thinking of
buying some boots."

"You? In boots?" She looked at me sideways.

"They're for dancing," I said.

"You're finally getting out of Phoenix, and now you want to look like everyone here?"

"I'm just trying to have a little fun before I have to button down." I tried to sound casual, though things with Buddy were anything but. "Just once" had fast become a habit, all the more irresistible because sneaking out to meet him was my way of stealing time.

"Fun?" said Rosa. "What's that?" Like me, she was working six days, some double shifts, at La Piñata or the hospital. "Maybe you can teach me," she added unexpectedly.

"About fun?"

"How to cowboy dance."

"I just follow," I said. "Buddy leads."

Rosa laughed and raised her sunglasses. "And you call yourself a feminist?" The word was Rosa's secret weapon. "What would Amanda have to say about that?"

I was relieved that her teasing had found its familiar target. "Anyway, you don't need me to teach you," I said. "I saw line dancing listed as a major in the Stanford catalog."

"You're minoring in Buddy, girlfriend. Maybe you should worry about where dancing with that guy will lead."

At Boots, Buddy and I practiced a tense step in the club's dark corners, one in which he pushed and I

resisted, saying, "Someone will see." He complained that the club was too noisy, too busy,
too public. He wanted to take me someplace
different, he said, someplace where we could be
alone.

Alone: the word made me wary.

Alone was Dad in prison, Mom up late answering
the questions in a sex survey in some women's magazine. *Alone* was me lying awake listening to Dad's car
in the driveway and then the sound of angry, sorry
voices behind a closed door. Fury and remorse was the
weird glue that held my parents together. I thought
alone was the inevitable consequence of their kind of
passion.

Rosa went into the apartment to refill our iced cof-
fees while I shuffled through the rest of my mail.
Grocery coupons, department store sale flyer, a letter
from A.S.U. addressed to my mom. The Bryn Mawr bill
was just behind it, requesting my contribution to
tuition, room, and board. I knew the figure by heart, by
dollars per hour, by how many plates of crab cakes and
crab mousse I would have to serve that summer to earn
it. I didn't need to be reminded. I put it aside and went
on.

American Teen magazine, an eighth-grade graduation gift from Grandma Cody. I let it drop to the damp
grass, watched the water splotch the cover model as
though she were diseased. No matter. I was way past
the problems those bright-colored pages promised to
solve.

A mail-order catalog, filled with rich-looking, unsmiling models wearing foody colors called "wheat," "butter," and "maize." Amanda's people probably looked like this, I thought, well-fed but still slender, smooth hair held back unnecessarily with pastel madras bands. Their even tans were a code for leisure that I was just beginning to understand. You didn't get that color catching sun slanting off the roof of an apartment building. And Rosa's skin, a permanent version of the same gold-brown shade, had an entirely different meaning. I tossed the catalog to the ground.

And finally, a letter for me from my father. I felt a pang as I examined his handwriting, the big, loopy circles, a generous embrace holding nothing but air. My fingers actually trembled as I held the tight little package. It was as excruciating as a kid's Christmas, the feeling of powerlessness in the face of possibility. It was safer not to open it.

"Anything good?" asked Rosa. I quickly hid Dad's letter at the bottom of the pile.

"Mom got something from A.S.U."

"You still think she wants you to stay in Arizona?"

"I hope not," I said. "She's been acting so weird lately, as if she's already decided he's guilty."

Rosa laid her hand on my arm. "Don't you? Jaime, he took your money."

At that moment, a swarm of cicadas hidden in the citrus trees revealed themselves, as if they sensed some danger in the cloudless sky. Their buzzing was frantic, like sizzling bacon. I stood up so quickly I saw stars.

"Let's go somewhere," I said, gathering up my stack of mail. "Let's go to the mall."

Rosa wrinkled her nose. The mall was the backdrop for many of our Worst Case Scenarios.

"I want those boots," I said.

"All right," she said, hauling herself out of the lounge chair. "Anything for air conditioning."

Inside, I went to the hall closet and retrieved the double-taped shoebox from behind a leaning tower of old board games. PRIVATE! PLEASE DON'T OPEN!!! I'd written in felt pen for Mom's prying eyes. This elaborate packaging was a decoy, advertising love letters from high school boys, which I knew my mother wouldn't touch. In fact, it was full of my father's unopened letters and my Future, Part Two.

"You're loco!" Rosa had said when she saw the money piled high inside the box. "You could be earning interest!"

"It's safer in that box than it is in the bank," I said. Every time I opened the box and saw those rolls of coins and banded stacks, I felt rich. When Rosa wasn't looking, I slipped Dad's letter under the pile of bills.

In Phoenix, you have to lay towels across the car seat all summer so you won't skin yourself alive. You can't even hold the steering wheel, it's so flaming hot—you have to tap it strategically to stay in your lane. In our

Pinto, there's a strip across the dashboard where the sun burned the vinyl pale. By noon, the entire interior is sticky, as though the car, at any moment, might ooze onto its tires.

Rosa covered her face with her hands as we turned into the Galleria, a crowd of sad old department stores with a bright, brand-new stucco facade. "I'm staying in Phoenix," she said, and our old joke was like a cold-air rush of relief. It couldn't happen, I told myself, so long as we could laugh about it.

"And dying of sunstroke," I said.

"So you're buried at Squaw Peak."

"In the picnic area, where my grave is defaced with corn chips and barbecue beans."

"And chewing tobacco."

"But marked with a fitting monument—Ben Franklin in a Stetson. In bronze."

"Then the developers come in, with an idea for a theme park."

"Liberty Land."

"The highway signs say 'Go east, young woman.'"

"The signs are mysterious."

"Stretching on for miles."

"Then when you get there, it's not a park at all, just this shop they charge admission for, full of miniature tomahawks and Zuni trolls."

"Wearing cowboy boots," said Rosa.

"That's not funny," I said.

*　　*　　*

My
Life
as a
girl

"So when are you going to introduce me?" Rosa asked as I stood before a knee-high mirror, admiring a pair of gray snakeskin boots.

With any luck? Never. "I don't know," I said. "Buddy sort of works weird hours."

"What does he do?" she said.

Buddy's job confused me, partly because it was difficult to picture him doing anything but dancing. "He test-drives cars," I said. I added, as if to give him status, "Sometimes he drives to San Diego."

"Hmm," Rosa said.

"Y'all need help?" said a Boot Barn salesman whose twang, I was sure, was a fake.

"I'll take these," I said decisively, one of the quickest purchases I had ever made.

The boots made a cricket-crunching sound as I walked stiffly to the counter. I hauled my backpack up to the counter, pulling out ten pounds of rolled quarters.

"Waitresses," the salesman muttered under his breath.

"I'll wear them out," I said.

I wore the boots exactly three times.

The last time, my heels were so blistered that Buddy had to carry me from his car back to our apartment. "Put me down, this is stupid," I said, but my feet were throbbing, and he'd parked farther away than he usually did. "Just hold on," he said. He started walking and I settled into him, wrapping my arms around his neck.

It was nearly three, and most of the houses on our block were darkened, the families inside having long ago gone to sleep. We trudged toward our apartment. I felt sad thinking of the darkened windows, the droning TV.

Just ahead a house was hosting a party. It was lit up like a jack-o'-lantern, with three tooth gaps at ground level and two wide-open eyes upstairs. "Stop here," I told Buddy. "I have to get these boots off."

He set me down gently on the sidewalk, but I nearly fell over trying to support myself on what felt like two balls of fire. "Let me help you," Buddy said.

A square of light fell through a first-floor window of the party house, throwing ghosts onto the silver lawn. "Relax," he whispered, setting me down and easing off my boots. He held my swollen feet in his lap, cuffed my jeans, and slowly peeled off my socks. "Okay?" he asked.

"Okay," I said.

First he blew on my feet to cool them, then stroked my arches, the bony knob of my big toe. He touched me without making me ticklish. I was paralyzed by how good it felt.

"We don't have to go dancing anymore," he whispered. "We can do other things."

I couldn't answer; a lump blocked my throat. I lay back on the grass and watched shadows pass the windows. I'd never noticed before how lamplight could reveal a house's skeleton, the way rooms were connected within its walls.

"Looks like a rocking party," Buddy said. "I wish we could go in."

"I don't," I croaked. "I like this, right here."

I tried to focus on the feeling of his fingers circling my arches, to try to keep myself from bursting into tears. There was nothing beautiful about the party house, I told myself. Except that it used to be ours.

"Jaime, are you crying?" Buddy asked me, gently setting my feet on the grass.

"No," I said, my voice cracking. "Yes. It just hurts so much."

Buddy stretched out next to me, then pulled my head to his chest and let me rest there. Beneath the wide night sky, I felt small and insignificant and grateful to have him to hold on to. I wanted to stay there forever, while my life hurtled forward.

chapter eleven

I missed every sunset that summer, only glimpsed them through the panoramic windows of The Phoenix dining room. The light faded from the sky so slowly I never actually saw it happen. I counted by minutes, dishes delivered, tip money made, the time until I would be released into air as hot as bathwater. Buddy would pull up to the Big Tree without his headlights, cruising like a big secret fish. One night. Five. Ten. Fifty. Time moved oddly in the middle of the night: not a line, but a net tangling together anger, sadness, love.

Sometimes we'd go dancing, but more often we'd just drive. Up Central, down Seventh, up Central again. Our real destination was a ratty blanket spread across a corner of the lawn at our old house. At some point, after we'd done enough laps around the track, we'd end up back there.

I loved kissing Buddy. I loved it so much that, at first, I believed I could know everything I needed to know about him by tasting the strawberry toothpaste he favored and breathing in the faint leather scent of

My
Life
as a
girl

his skin. I knew that he loved me and wanted me to love him. I knew by the way his hands rested lightly, patiently, on my shoulders that he wouldn't rush me. But what I thought I knew I only imagined. You can imagine anything when your eyes are closed. That must be the reason for kissing.

"How old were you when your father left?" I asked Buddy one night, as if his answer would let me know him well enough.

"I don't know—eight," he said.

I remembered Shelly's tip tray, the photo of Buddy as a kid. "That's so sad," I said. "When I was that age, I couldn't get to sleep unless someone tucked me in."

Buddy scooted closer, followed the line of my collarbone with his lips. "I still can't," he said.

"Buddy, I'm serious. Did you miss him?" I thought of Dad's empty place at the table, holidays minus his rowdy unchecked joy, Mom sleeping alone in that Great Plains of beds. He wouldn't see me off to college, might not even see me graduate.

Buddy frowned. "I don't remember. Why are you hung up on my old man?"

"I'm just curious," I said. He closed his eyes, but I'd already seen the BOYS ONLY sign he'd put up.

After one of Dad's trips to Las Vegas, I'd sat with him in the kitchen, admiring the leather coat he'd bought for Mom to keep himself from throwing away the prize. He was a generous thief at least, squandering money and love as if the supply were endless, while Mom pursed her lips and put the coat away in a closet. Of course I loved him more.

"I love you," I said to Buddy one night as we drank beer from greasy glasses at Boots. The words had appeared in my head and I spent them, as if to reassure myself that I could.

Buddy laughed. "No, you don't," he said. "Not yet."

I punched him in the shoulder. "What makes you so sure?"

"You're careful," he said. "Like how you dance."

Mom insisted on driving every morning to El Rancho, though I was the one dropping her off. The way she white-knuckled the steering wheel annoyed me. I wanted to scream, listening to the sandpaper slide as the wheel moved beneath her calloused hands.

"Where's your wedding ring?" I asked her one morning.

She looked down at her fingers. "In a safe place," she said.

"You think he's guilty."

"That's enough of your lip, young lady."

Buddy parked next door to our old house, and we started down the darkened street as cautiously as burglars. The neighborhood was silent except for the clunk-scrape of Buddy's boots on asphalt. I was relieved when we reached the soft cover of lawn.

My

Life

as a

girl

That's when the car came around the corner, its headlights flashing suddenly across the facade. Buddy and I dove into the overgrown oleanders at the side of the house and crouched there, chins pressed against our knees, among the toxic blossoms.

"It's your Pinto," Buddy whispered, peeking through a branch of the bush.

"You're kidding!" I said. "My mom?" I started to laugh, nervous little barking noises, and Buddy reached over and squeezed my hand. "Maintain, would you?" he snapped.

"Oh, God, she sees us," I whispered as the Pinto turned into the driveway. I let my knees buckle to the cool mud and listened as the car door opened and Mom walked across the lawn. She passed right by us on her way to the gate. I could see that she was barefoot, wearing her terry cloth robe.

"What's she doing?" I whispered, and Buddy shook his head. But when Mom unlatched the gate and went into the yard, I wrestled my way out of the bushes and silently followed.

I watched from behind the fence as Mom tiptoed across the pool deck and climbed onto the diving board. She stood at the edge of the board lightly bouncing. A snake from the pool cleaner broke the dark surface of the water, making a lone, sad-sounding splash.

Mom raised her arms to dive and then lowered them, trying it on again and again. Finally, she paused and unbelted her robe. As it dropped to the deck, I was relieved to see that, beneath it, she wore her swimsuit.

Behind me, Buddy whispered, "Let's book, Jaime. Before she gets caught."

I hadn't realized he was watching. When he spoke, I felt my mother's nakedness, saw her private longing and grief exposed. I turned away quickly. When I heard the splash, I was already running fast, fast to Buddy's car.

chapter

twelve

It was the heat that drove me to do it, to gamble with my job at The Phoenix for a dip in that blue sparkling pool. I took Buddy with me. We carried a pair of blue bath towels bought at JCPenney, a color I hoped was close enough to the hotel's royal blue.

"Try to act unimpressed," I whispered to Buddy as he unlatched the fancy wrought-iron gate. The towels were meant to make us look like paying customers. The finishing touch to our disguise was a wealthy attitude.

But even Buddy, who'd called The Phoenix "butt-ugly" when I first met him, whistled under his breath. "Man, just look at this place."

It was pretty amazing. The pool area was made to look like Maui, with palm trees, blue-green water, and a moss-covered slide. Glancing around, I remembered the day I'd first seen it, when I'd taken the restaurant exam. That day, Rosa had helped me study for the job that Buddy might now help me lose.

We made our way to two lounge chairs and tried to look bored as we spread out our towels. From behind my sunglasses, my eyes searched the area: men and women sunning, reading, being served sandwiches by waiters clad in white shorts and polos. There were a few pale couples who looked as if they'd been pried away from fluorescent-lit offices for vacations their doctors prescribed. But most had the studied grace and prettiness of people who spent half their lives in hotel suites, salon chairs, and tanning booths, checking out the people who are checking them out.

"Might as well get wet," Buddy said, his face disappearing into his shirt. I only knew parts of his body (his hands, thick wrists, salty brown neck, the V of chest exposed by his unbuttoned shirt) and usually by touch, in the dark. Now, suddenly, I was face to face with his muscular belly, the downy blond hair above the waistband of his red swimsuit. In broad daylight. I didn't know where to look.

"You go ahead," I said, arranging myself carefully on the chair. "I'm going to fry first." I felt shy with Buddy suddenly. What had I been thinking when I'd put on this bikini?

Buddy dove into the water without even dipping a toe in to test it. It wasn't a show-off dive, though, like the cannonballs of boys at the public pool. He went into the water cleanly. When he poked his head up in the deep end, he motioned to me.

"Quit your grilling, and come on in!" he called.

I looked around quickly, and raised a finger to my lips. I didn't want to attract attention. There were wait-

My
Life

as a

girl

ers around, none of whom I recognized, but who knew if my boss, Ms. Pickett, sometimes took her break by the pool?

Buddy swam to the poolside and put his elbows on the deck. With his hair wet, his eyes burned blue in his head. "You must be a chimichanga by now," he said. "Come get cool."

"Any minute now," I said, paralyzed by sudden self-consciousness. He was right, though; the sun was making me dizzy. So was watching a man next to me rub coconut-scented sunblock on his girlfriend's back in long, sleepy strokes. *Soon*, I said to myself. *Not yet.*

I closed my eyes and thought of pool parties we'd had when I was a little girl. Neighborhood kids and cousins played Marco Polo while the grownups stood waist-deep in water, cocktail glasses in hand. Drinking, I had noticed, always made people loud, talking not so others could hear them but so they could hear themselves.

I'd be quietly treading water around the kid who was "it" when some friend of my father's would almost blow my cover, pushing his shiny, scary face up to mine. "This your kid? She's a heartbreaker, just like her dad." The word confused me; was it a compliment or a curse? I'd let my breath out and sink to the bottom, where I wouldn't have to answer, where it was so quiet I imagined I heard ice cubes tinkling against glass. I believed then that if I sank in one end of the pool and emerged in the other, no one would recognize me.

Now a shadow moved across my eyelids, interrupting my daydream. I opened my eyes and turned my head. My vision followed jerkily.

"Buddy?" I said.

A different guy's voice said, "May I bring you something to drink?"

It was a young-looking guy in a white uniform, an embroidered phoenix bird on his sleeve. His face didn't look familiar, but he looked as if he knew me.

"Oh," I said, feeling dazed as I hauled myself up. "Yes. How about a glass of iced tea?" The way he was staring made me panic for a moment. Forgetting my bikini, I got off the chaise and started toward the pool.

"Room number?" the waiter said.

I turned slowly and stared at him, uncomprehending. Whoever had dressed this boy in authority had clearly misjudged his size. His neck bulged and blushed against his collar, and he kept shifting his body from his left foot to his right. "It's printed on your room key," he said, blocking my path to the water.

"My room key." Of course, the room key was the real proof. If you didn't have it, blue towels and blasé didn't count for much.

"Uh, if you're a guest," he said, licking his bottom lip nervously, "you should have one." Finally, he withdrew his outstretched hand, so certain was he that I didn't have the goods. "Jaime, we took the test together," he whispered. "Don't you remember me?"

Then I heard a voice behind me, a woman's voice I recognized as well as the *tap-tap* of her tiny high heels.

My
Life
as a
girl

"I thought so," said Ms. Pickett, *tap-tap-tap-tap*. "Jaime, may I see you in my office?"

I didn't answer her. Without really thinking, I dove into the pool.

"I'm waiting," said Ms. Pickett after I came to the surface. Behind her, our Penney's towels stuck out like amateur artwork, an inferior blueberry blue. I treaded water in a circle, turning counterclockwise to follow her poolside patrol. I half-feared she'd get a net and try to fish me out.

By that point, we had an audience. Swimmers stopped midstroke to gawk at us. Sunbathers put down their paperbacks, sneaking peeks over tan-tinted lenses. They seemed to be waiting to see what I'd do.

What choice did I have? Buddy had abandoned me. Ms. Pickett was going to fire me, in the water or out of it. From the look on her face, I could see she was savoring the thought of booting me out of Maui-land and back to the classifieds.

She was at the steps now, crouching and beckoning. "Jaime," she warned me impatiently, her makeup melting in the heat like grilled cheese. "We don't want to make a scene."

I breaststroked to the poolside, ready to give myself up. But when she reached out her jeweled hand to help me, I jerked back instinctively. I sank underwater and pushed off the wall with both feet. When I came up for air, I was swimming at full speed.

"Whoo!" I heard someone scream.

"Go, girl!" said another.

It wasn't their cheering that kept me going; it was the thought of what I'd done. Shame had always been my fuel. Because Dad couldn't keep an honest job, I got perfect grades in school. Because he left his living to chance, I would make mine through science. I saved my money for the future because he flashed ours around and lost it like a fool. I could go all the way to Bryn Mawr running on shame's fumes.

You blew it, you blew it, you blew it, I chanted underwater as my limbs sliced up the pool. For letting Dad take my money in the first place, and now for risking my job. Arms punching, feet slapping, I pulled through the water, feeling shame leave my body like rocket parts, spent energy. I swam until I was angry, and then on until my anger trailed behind me like a burnt-orange flame.

When I came up for air in the shallow end, I felt unrecognizable, the way I'd wished to feel as a kid. I had my anger back, that was part of it, and I felt myself move more determinedly. With Buddy, I'd been stuck in soft-blur daydreams, but now I zoomed back to sharp reality. If I could get out of this situation somehow, I promised myself, I would stop fooling around with Buddy. I would do it today.

Exhausted, I waded toward the pool steps, which were curved and stacked like wedding cake. At the top, Ms. Pickett and Buddy waited, looking like a judge and a shotgun bridegroom. Buddy had changed into his shorts again and wore a bright green Phoenix polo. So he'd been inside buying souvenirs while I was outside paying for what we'd done.

Still, I accepted the Phoenix towel he offered, let him wrap me up in the right color blue. Under the terry cloth cover, he squeezed my hand.

"Nice shirt," I said, curling my fingers into a fist.

He looked at Ms. Pickett, then looked at me. He said, "There's one for you in our room."

"Your room?" asked Ms. Pickett.

"West wing," said Buddy, casually taking the key from his pocket and swinging it around on its phoenix bird chain. "A really classy view."

I was so stunned I was speechless. A minute before, I'd been guilty; now I was…not quite innocent, but legitimate. Buddy had either stolen a key or rented a room.

Ms. Pickett examined the key for a moment, turning it twice in her palm. I thought for a moment she would bite it, to ensure its authenticity.

"Would you mind taking our picture?" asked Buddy, handing Ms. Pickett a disposable camera. "We're on our honeymoon."

"Excuse me," she said, looking embarrassed. "It's just that you're so young." I was still trying to figure out what had happened as Ms. Pickett snapped a photograph of the two of us crushed against the plastic palms.

"How did you do that?" I whispered as Buddy walked me through the lobby to the elevator.

"Shhh," he said, wrapping an arm around my waist. When the doors closed safely behind us, he kissed me as though we truly were newlyweds. Then the elevator opened at the fourth floor, and I saw that Buddy really had done it. He'd rented the bridal suite.

The room was blinding white, all wispy tulle and satin moiré. The ceiling was done up like frosting, with stiff waves of plaster like some sugary whipped dessert. "It's so white," I said while Buddy and I stood stunned at the threshold.

"Like church," Buddy said.

A bellboy pushed past us then with a bouquet of white lilies in a silver vase. He put these on the dresser, then waited awkwardly for his tip. Finally, Buddy palmed him a dollar, then lifted me in my towel and carried me in. Then he set me down on the thick, white carpet that gave like soft sand under my bare feet.

"This must have cost a fortune," I said.

"Yeah," said Buddy. "It did."

I couldn't help touching things as I wandered around the room. The chilled crystal pitcher, the velvet table skirt, the quilted satin bedspread were all so different from the lived-in luxury of the Gutierrez house. The wintry beauty of the hotel room whispered, "I made it on my own."

"It's pretty," I admitted.

"So are you," Buddy said.

I'd been tracing the lace on the tablecloth, but now

I pulled my hand away, tried to remember the promise I'd made to myself in the pool. "Buddy," I scolded. "You didn't need to rescue me."

"What was *your* plan? Swim to Mexico?"

"I was going to turn myself in."

"And lose your job?"

"Yes!" I said. "No. Maybe not. I can't afford to. But I also can't afford this."

"It's taken care of," Buddy said, grabbing a green champagne bottle from where it nested in a bucket of ice. "So why don't we just kick back and have fun?" With his teeth, Buddy peeled the foil wrapper back, and pressed his thumb against the cork. When it blew, he caught the airy liquid in two crystal flutes.

"The way I see it, you've got lots to celebrate. One," he said, handing me a glass, "you've still got your job. Two"—he took a gulp—"we've got air conditioning and MTV. And three"—he pushed off his shoes and sat down on the king-sized bed.

"It's cold in here," I said, rubbing my arms. Underneath my towel skirt, my bathing suit was still damp.

Buddy pulled back the bedspread and said, "Come on in, then, and get warm."

As I stood there, I heard someone knocking. "Oh, Lord, it's Ms. Pickett," I said. "I might as well just tell her the truth."

Buddy didn't seemed surprised or afraid, though. He called out, "Come in!" A waiter wheeled in a cart piled high with dome-covered dishes. "Here's dinner," Buddy said. "Why don't you at least eat, before you confess?"

He'd ordered up oysters with salsa and cilantro, a basket of fresh-baked blue corn bread, a salad scattered with rose petals and—the most expensive item on our menu—medallions of buffalo.

It was the dinner I'd served to others all summer, finally being served to me. I was starving. I felt my resolve escape as quickly as the steam from these dishes as Buddy dramatically lifted each lid.

"One hundred twenty with tax and tip," I calculated as Buddy placed a plate in front of me. "Buddy, where will you get the money for all this?"

"I'll call in a debt," he said, picking up a tiny silver fork. "Here, have an oyster," he said, poking at the grayish meat and lifting it to my lips.

I made a face. "I grew up in the desert!" I said, to explain my squeamishness.

"So did I."

"So when did you become a seafood connoisseur?"

"I used to go fishing in San Diego with my dad," he said. "We'd be out there all day and not catch a thing. Then we'd stop by these shacks that sell oysters dredged up from the bay."

While Buddy was talking, I thought of a baseball glove Dad had oiled for me, his Saturday work shirt, dried petals from the graduation bouquet he'd ordered from jail. I'd been hoarding these things even while I stashed away his unopened letters and refused to visit.

My
Life
as a

girl

Regardless of what the jury decided, I felt I had to choose between my dad or my life.

"Just taste it," said Buddy, reaching over and placing an open-faced shell on my plate. "You'll never know if you don't."

I prodded the oyster with the fork Buddy handed me and started to saw it in half.

"Pick it up whole," he said, "and put it on your tongue."

"Whole? You don't cut it?"

"No, you sort of—inhale," he said.

He speared another oyster and let it slide down his gullet like a trained seal. The sight of the lump moving down his throat nauseated me. Still, I raised the gray blob to my mouth.

"Wait," Buddy said in the nick of time, before it passed my teeth. "I forgot to say don't chew."

"Don't chew?" I said. "What's the point of eating them if you don't even get to chew?"

"Just taste it," he said.

At first it felt slimy, like mucus, and I wanted to cough it up. But I let it sit on my tongue for a minute, and—behind all that salsa and cilantro—I began to taste the sea. I wasn't sure I liked it, but it was certainly mysterious. After all, I told myself as I swallowed, that's where new tastes come from: out of what at first seems foreign or dangerous or out of one's reach.

"You like it?" Buddy said hopefully as I reached for another piece of oyster meat.

"I need to try it again to know what I think," I said.

He smiled. "That's the spirit," he said.

The Sonoran pool was a different island altogether in the evening. The green glowing pool light made the water seem unreal and our bodies as white as pickled cabbage. As Buddy and I waded in, the water sent up a clean scent of chlorine that made my limbs relax. We were the only two people in the pool.

An abandoned raft floated near us in the water, and I paddled over to it and hoisted half my body up, resting my head on my crossed arms. Buddy joined me on the raft, wrapping his arms around mine, letting his chest rest weightlessly against my back. "That's nice," I said, closing my eyes.

We drifted that way for a long while, rocking gently, listening to the water gurgling in the filter and lapping quietly against the ceramic border tiles. I was so full and sleepy and grateful to Buddy for helping me keep my job. I loved the feeling of his body around me, the way he kissed my cheek, my nose, my jawbone gently, affectionately, as though I were a sleeping child.

Then I felt his hand slide around my hip to my belly, and down, across the elastic border of my bathing suit. I kept my eyes closed, like a cheater, not stirring as he moved his fingers in circles slowly, expertly. A part of me felt embarrassed that he knew just where to touch me, and just how it would feel. He knew, too, that when I let out my breath and shuddered, it was over. And knowing that meant he had me.

Afterward, I slid underwater and swam to the deep end. Buddy followed me. I hated the smug, sexy smile on his face when he came up for air, the way he panted like an animal, trying to catch his breath. "Jaime," he said, "how long are you going to make me wait?"

I gasped at the unexpected question, and sank back down to the bottom of the pool. My breath escaped in bubbles, like ballast released. Above me, Buddy's legs were magnified by the pool light, dangling larger than life. I watched them scissor in the water as he sank to join me. I shook my head, and he reached out to catch my billowing hair, trying to wind it around his hand.

The weird light made me feel as if we were encased in clear jelly—safe, unmoving, timeless. Then my chest began to ache. I pushed myself back up to the surface, and when my head broke the water's seal, he was still waiting. "Come on, Jaime," he begged.

"Buddy, I can't."

He treaded water. "Are you afraid?" he asked.

"Of course not," I said, then added, "Should I be?"

"I'll be so careful," he said. He grabbed me and kissed me, his mouth tasting warm and chalky, like chlorine. "Jaime, I've never wanted anyone so much in my whole life."

"I want you, too," I said, but I didn't, not really, not

the way he meant. I loved kissing him, hearing his breath change, the private excitement of getting so close. I would have waited there forever, next to the room where doors slammed and accusations flew.

"I just want it to be special," I said, fishing for lines I'd read in a book.

"What?" said Buddy, chopping at the water angrily with his open hand. "This"—he indicated the hotel—"isn't special enough?"

"Oh, I get it," I answered angrily. "You didn't get the room to help me keep my job. It was just a trick to get me into bed."

"A trick?" Buddy pulled himself out of the water, bringing a wave of water with him and slopping up the deck. "Jaime, you don't even know what you want."

I swam to the pool edge and sat there hugging my knees on the wedding cake steps. "You don't know what I want," I said. "You wouldn't even understand."

Buddy walked along the pool's edge, triggering the sensor-controlled patio lights all along the deck. He yelled, "You're into it, Jaime, I know you are. What just happened out there on the raft?"

"Buddy, be quiet!" I screamed at him, but he kept on pacing, his steps spotlit on the stage that was the pool deck.

"You think that you're too good for me?" he shouted back. Then he stormed off to the lobby, flinging water in front of him, with someone else's towel around his neck.

My

Life

as a

girl

I sat there on the steps for a long time, watching my toes in the water. But when another couple waded in, giggling and murmuring, I began to feel like a voyeur. I took the key Buddy had forgotten and went back to our empty bridal suite. There, I called the one person I knew I could count on to come and rescue me.

While I waited for Rosa, I took one last look around the suite, checked the drawer for the Gideon Bible and the closet for Buddy's clothes, which were gone. There were two chilled chocolate coins waiting on the pillows. I pocketed these, as well as some scented soaps and shampoo from the bathroom, the complimentary lilies from the crystal vase, and a stack of hotel stationery embossed with a gold phoenix bird. Then I sat down at the white enamel desk and began to write a letter to my Bryn Mawr roommate, Amanda, describing my romantic weekend away with the boy of my dreams.

chapter
thirteen

"I thought you weren't allowed to use the pool," Rosa said as I climbed into her front seat.

"Buddy rented a room," I muttered, and she looked at me as if I were a stranger. Up to that point, Rosa's suspicions had been phantoms, ringing the bell and disappearing. Now, as she picked me up at a hotel and took in my wet hair and soaked clothes, I watched her answer the door and let the idea in: *Buddy and Jaime are sleeping together.*

"Jaime, what do you see in him?" she asked.

"Buddy's friends ask him the same question," I said. "Why does he keep hanging out with me, since I won't have sex with him?"

"Well, they're pigs," said Rosa, though I could tell she was relieved. "Buddy should kiss your feet."

"He's a good guy," I said. I could feel my face unraveling, drooping grotesquely into one of those tragedy masks.

"Why are you defending him," asked Rosa, "after what he did?"

"He needs me. I can't just stand by and let him fall."

"Yes," said Rosa firmly. "You can." She leaned across me, fishing a tissue out of the glove compartment for me to use to blow my nose.

We drove in silence the rest of the way to my apartment, until Rosa turned the corner and both of us gasped out loud. 4-EVR was sprayed in black paint across the stucco front of our apartment building.

"He wouldn't," said Rosa, stopping at the curb.

"Can't he even spell?" I added, before Rosa had a chance.

Inside, Mom's sisters Henri and Jo Ellen were at the kitchen table, which was littered with dinner dishes, wrapping paper, and wineglasses, the remains of a celebration I had obviously missed.

I tried to hurry past them to my bedroom, calling out over my shoulder, "I'm home! I just have to get changed."

"Jaime, come here," Mom said, in a brittle voice. Had she seen Buddy's love note? If her sisters had driven from the farm in Yuma, they had to have been there for a couple of hours.

I stopped in the doorway, and Mom said, "Where have you been?"

"Swimming," I said.

"Swimming," Henri repeated, curling a piece of hair around her finger. She looked over at Jo Ellen and smiled. I loved my aunts, but when they were together, they had a weird power. They could read your mind, they would open your mail. They loomed large in my letters to Amanda. I just wished they didn't loom so large in my life.

"Sit down," said Jo Ellen, pushing a plate of untouched food toward me. "You must be starving."

"You were with that boy," said Mom.

"What boy?" I said, inching away from the table.

"You know perfectly well what boy," she said.

Jo Ellen crushed her cigarette into her own empty plate and leaned toward me. "Jaime isn't eating," she said.

"Jaime is full," I said.

"It's that boy," Mom said. "I knew it from the minute I laid eyes on him."

"What boy?" said Henri, picking up her wineglass with hands like paddles at the end of her slender wrists.

"That Buddy boy."

"Ah, yes," Henri said. "The boy with the hat." Mom had examined the hat again and again, not knowing what to make of it.

"What did that boy do to you?" Mom asked.

"Nothing," I said. "We had a fight." I pushed my chair back from the table and halfway stood.

"Sit down," said Jo Ellen. "You're not going to waste away to nothing over some boy."

"Let her be," said Henri, nodding as she spoke. It worked like hypnosis; the other sisters nodded along and backed off.

"Did you tell her?" asked Jo Ellen, picking up an envelope on the table, and Mom said, "Later." I didn't want to know the reason for the celebration, but I had a creepy feeling it had to do with Dad's demise.

"Tomatoes!" Henri said suddenly, and Jo Ellen sprang up from her chair. "I'll bring them in," she told my mother. "We brought you a bushel, ripened on the vine."

I fled to take a shower. If they hadn't seen Buddy's message before, they would surely see it now.

Later, I found Mom alone in the kitchen, kneeling in a four-foot circle of fresh tomato juice. There were smashed tomatoes everywhere: splattered on the bottom cabinets, leaking into the linoleum tile, rolling out of a sopping grocery bag. She looked angry, swirling the mess around on the floor with a juice-bloated sponge. The whole room smelled pungent and ripe.

"Whoa," I said from the dining area, a peninsula of olive-green carpet, juice lapping at its shore. "What happened?"

"I lifted the bag and it broke," Mom said. "Jo should know ripe tomatoes will rot sitting in the car on such a hot day."

Trying to be funny, I said, "Just ask Spider Reid."

Exasperated, Mom pointed at me with a dripping finger. "Did you see what that boy did to the front of the building?"

"I'll pay to have it sandblasted," I said.

"You bet your butt you will. By the way, in case you're interested, I got my acceptance today from A.S.U."

"Congratulations," I said halfheartedly.

Mom frowned and went back to mopping. "You're not the only one who can make a fresh start."

She wrung out the sponge in a cleaning bucket beside her, then slipped and fell on her butt in the juice. She had tomato seeds caught in her hair, and seeing these made me feel desperate. There was nothing I could say. At that moment, I would have done anything to rewind the last twenty-four hours, to erase what Buddy had written, to erase him altogether.

That night, I lay awake listening to the ticking of my windup alarm clock, waiting for Buddy's apology. I half-expected to see a shadow of his Stetson cast through my window onto the wall. The idea thrilled me. Finally, he rapped on the window glass, low and steady.

"Jaime, please, let me in," he said when I opened the window. He stood knee-deep in the baby palms that bordered my room.

"Go away," I said.

"Come on, Jaime," he said, shoving his fists into his pockets and stamping his feet on the ground for effect. He understood he was supposed to be impatient, and that I was supposed to make him wait. "It's hot out here," he pleaded.

My Life

as a

girl

I let him in then, pulling him feet first through the window and bringing in the desert dust and heat. "You're not even sorry," I said, but quietly, so as not to wake Mom, asleep in the room next door.

"I *am* sorry," he said. He pulled me close, pressing against my thin nightgown. "I was pissed," he said.

"My mother saw it," I said. "She's suspicious enough as it is."

"I didn't mean it."

"What do you mean, you didn't mean it?" I was so caught up in the indignation I'd rehearsed, I couldn't remember where my question had been leading. I wasn't sure what I wanted to hear.

I watched as he peeled off his shirt, tossing it onto my night table, covering a pamphlet Mom had placed there: "Are You Ready for Love?" He kept glancing at my bedroom door, as though the flimsy nipple lock could keep our secret. "I'll pay for it," he said finally, sitting down on the edge of my bed.

"You bet your butt you will," I said.

I climbed into bed and pulled the covers tight around me, wanting somehow to prolong his apology. "It happened to my mother once," I told him.

"Yeah?" he said, struggling out of his boots.

"His name was Spider," I said. "And believe me, my mother was furious." But I had already tried on fury earlier, at the pool, and it had looked ridiculous. With relief and a little disappointment, it occurred to me that the time for being angry at Buddy had already come and gone.

"Well, you're not at all like your mother," he said, setting his boots side by side by the door.

"Why did you do it?" I asked. I still wanted to believe his desire for me was complicated, and that what I wanted from him was simple: a boy's arms around me in the dark.

He said, "Because I want you. I mean, I just want to hold you. I promise." He kissed me as though he meant it, and said over and over how sorry he was. He stroked my shoulders, making circles, until I wasn't aware of his hands so much as the movement. It would take years, I thought sadly as I lay there with Buddy, before the wind and rain washed away Buddy's love note completely. And I would be a different person then.

chapter

fourteen

My last day at The Phoenix was as anonymous as any visitor's. I cleaned my last table, picked up my paycheck, and walked unnoticed through the shimmering lobby one last time. At Franklin's, my leaving was more festive, coinciding with the diner's annual All-You-Can-Eat Fish Fry.

That morning, I found Casey and Shelly hanging red and white streamers from the ceiling, and another waitress named Estil tying blue balloons to the back of a booth. Casey motioned to the front window, to where a crowd was already gathered. "Check out these All-You-Can-Eaters!" she said. "These guys need bibs to catch their drool."

By eleven, when we opened, the line was backed up to the parking lot with impatient customers. Our regulars were the worst of the lot, scowling and elbowing newcomers, as though familiarity with the diner gave them some greater claim. Natives and newcomers alike clutched newspaper coupons with the same frantic-making, fine-print disclaimer: FIRST COME, FIRST SERVED.

"Ready?" Kenny asked us, his master key poised. Watching his pantomime, the line charged the door.

"Look at them," said Estil, backing away. "They're frightening."

"They're hungry," I said.

"Get a life," said Casey. "If I had the day off, I'd be at Big Surf."

"Ken, remind me why we're doing this?" asked Shelly. "I haven't forgotten last year's crab fiasco."

"Don't get me started," said Casey.

"Oh, Lord," said Estil, biting her nails.

"What's crab fiasco?" I asked. "Is that a new dish?"

But Kenny had already unlocked and opened the door. In flowed the ravenous crowd.

"Wake me when they've ordered," said Estil, running for the kitchen.

Shelly, on the other hand, faced the wave head-on. She expertly directed traffic at her station, taking food orders like tolls. "Crab? Shrimp? Clam?" she asked each customer before she'd let them through. "Crab? Shrimp? Clam?"

"Follow me," Casey bravely commanded with a beckoning sweep of her arm.

Good, I thought, let her take the hungriest customers, the ones who'd arrived early or shoved their way to the front. In the spirit of all-you-can-eat, they'd send her scrambling to and from the kitchen all day. But Casey passed right by her own station. Instead, she lured the group to my tables and then quickly abandoned them.

"Thanks, Case," I called to her as I hustled to the kitchen to get water.

"No prob," she said.

Shelly grabbed me then and led me to the break room, where she and Kenny had laid out a surprise going-away feast. I slid into the chair just as Estil and Shelly raised their iced tea glasses. "Good luck at Bryn Mawr," they said in unison.

"It's too bad, though," Kenny added, winking. "I had big plans for you."

"You're not the only one," said Shelly. Though I'd given Kenny two weeks' notice, I hadn't planned to tell Buddy I was leaving. Now, for the first time, I knew that Shelly knew about us.

"Casey's taking your tables," said Kenny, setting down a platter heaped with bay-seasoned crab. "So it's all you can eat"—he looked at his watch—"in twenty minutes."

"Fresh?" I asked, incredulous, as he passed out tiny mallets for crushing the shells.

"Try to keep it a secret," he stage-whispered, glancing over his shoulder as he spoke. "Or you'll have customers rioting in the kitchen trying to eat off your plate."

"Crab fiasco," I said.

"You got it," said Estil.

"Kenny—thank you," I said.

"My pleasure," he said, and disappeared into his office.

Our customers got mostly cornmeal batter for their nine ninety-nine, but we were dining like royalty. And though the meal was delicious, I picked at my food. "Eat up," Estil prodded me, but the thought of having to tell Buddy I was leaving before Shelly did had spoiled my appetite.

That day, for once we didn't eighty-six on tartar sauce. And people didn't linger as they usually did, asking for extra oyster crackers and one hundred tea refills. They ate, paid their bills, and got out like model customers. You could say it was a textbook fish fry, save for one tense ten-minute period when there were no clean forks to be found.

"That was easy," said Estil as we wiped down our tables.

"Yeah," said Casey. "What went wrong?"

On my way to the kitchen, the Hobart nearly hit me, screeching out the swinging door. "Jeez—slow down!" I said.

He smiled for the first time since I'd started, and raised a high-five. "I'm outta here," he said. "Par-tay!"

I didn't like the Hobart, but he had a wretched job, wearing a rubber apron and acting as a backstop for hurled dishes and half-eaten food. In a belated show of camaraderie, I slapped his soap-chapped hand.

In the kitchen, as I loaded empty glasses on a giant oval tray, I felt something tug at my apron strings.

My
Life

as a

girl

Warm breath steamed my neck as two tan arms slipped around my waist.

"Buddy!" I said sharply, upsetting the tray. Eighteen glasses clinked together like a curtain of crystal beads. As I turned, he peeled off my apron and tossed it to the floor. "I came to take you away," he said.

That's how we ended up cruising Central Avenue in a gray Mercedes, the latest and most elegant car Buddy was being paid to test. At first, he drove the car carefully, like a grandfather, until we came upon the entrance to I-17. Without warning, he turned north onto the freeway and stepped on the gas.

"Where are we going?" I asked him.

Buddy nodded. "How about if we just drive—see where we land?"

"Okay," I said.

In all my years in Arizona, I'd only been north twice. For vacation, my family preferred to drive south to Nogales to buy cheap liquor, or to drive the six hours west to Disneyland, intoxicated with junk food. Once, we'd almost gotten to the Grand Canyon, but then had taken a detour to Las Vegas instead. I went back with Rosa the day after graduation, because she said I wasn't allowed to go east for college until I could say I'd been there.

That summer, I always felt I should be elsewhere. Even my thoughts raced past my first semester at Bryn Mawr, past Dad's trial and the verdict, to the void that was afterward. But that afternoon, as I watched the landscape outside my window change from scrubby desert to sweet-smelling pine, I was happily suspended between the past and the future. Buddy and I drove for a while without a destination, without really talking, and an unexpected calm came over me.

I looked over at him, studying the tendons in his forearms, his naked Adam's apple, the hair curling over his collar. Because I was leaving, and because he didn't know it, I put my hand over his on the steering wheel and said, "This was a good idea."

Buddy smiled. "You know, Jim's got a cabin somewhere up here. Prescott, I think, is what he said."

That's when I knew that we'd been heading all along for a bedroom in a dark, damp cabin in Prescott for which Buddy already had precise directions and the front door key. He reached over and handcuffed my thigh with his fingers. I slumped in my seat and adjusted the air-conditioning vents so that they blasted directly at me.

Then I saw a sign advertising PIONEER VILLAGE eight miles farther north. "That looks interesting," I said, trying not to sound frantic. "Let's stop there. The exit's coming up."

Buddy had been the poster boy for patience, but now the odometer had crept up to seventy-five. "You're kidding, right?" he said. "It's like some kiddie amusement park."

"It's living history," I said, scanning the sign.

My
Life
as a
girl

"Come on, it'll be fun."

Reluctantly he exited, muttering to himself as pea gravel shot and pinged off the Mercedes in the parking lot. "One hundred, two hundred, three hundred," Buddy said as each granite missile hit.

"What are you counting?" I asked him.

"Bucks for a new paint job," he said. He parked in the shadow of a Desert Valley school bus and gave the car a once-over. When he'd concluded there was no damage, we bought our tickets and entered Pioneer Village between two Conestoga wagons.

Buddy hooked his hand in my back pocket the way junior high kids do at the mall. I let him. I was thinking that soon I would put him away in my scrapbook, board a plane, and refer to him affectionately as my summer romance. Buddy, of course, had a different idea.

In the first diorama we came to, a smithy forged horseshoes with a steel mallet and andiron. Though he tried to engage a tour group of grade schoolers in discussion, they just giggled and pointed to the apron he wore. Next door, at the post office, I bought a postcard showing a covered wagon at sunset. I started to write out a message to Rosa, then decided to save it for Amanda instead.

In the Pioneer Village jail, a clownish guy chuckled and hiccuped corn whiskey, bragging about stealing a chicken from the Widow Williams's yard. "So hang me," he said defiantly, nodding his head toward the gallows. "It's a much better view of the town." The line got fresh laughter from every new audience. It was strange to me that the site meant to house Pioneer Village's vices was also intended for comic relief.

"This is twisted," Buddy said as we headed for the next stall.

"Where's your sense of humor?" I asked.

At a campsite, a woman stirred a steaming pot over a fire while two little girls sat at her feet, playing with dolls made from muslin rags.

"I'm hungry," Buddy whispered, watching. "Do you think there's anything here to eat?" I stayed and listened politely to a speech about tortilla making while Buddy disappeared around the corner. He returned with two plates of Indian fry bread smothered with cowboy beans, straight out of Worst Case Scenario. I sunk my teeth into the soggy bread and found, to my surprise, it was delicious. Still, on principle, I tossed it into the next trash can I saw.

In the spirit of free enterprise, Pioneer Village offered an Indian bazaar. We wandered past tables displaying doll-sized pieces of pottery, turquoise jewelry, painted leather hair ornaments. Tense-looking customers wandered from table to table calculating, trying to decide which part of the Western experience they were going to take home. I tried not to notice as Buddy picked up a silver ring, turned it over to look at the price tag, then set it down again.

We came to a tiered display of kachina dolls, hundreds of brightly painted and feathered wood figures,

My
Life

as a

girl

their beady eyes staring straight ahead. "Two hundred fifty?" said a woman in dangling turquoise earrings and a leathery tourist tan. She enunciated carefully to be sure she was understood by the Native American woman who stood behind the counter. "For a piece of painted balsa?"

I found Buddy again at the entrance to the Living History Show. He surprised me by saying, "Let's go in."

The theater was a kind of chapel, with split logs for seats. There were seven other people in the audience. We found our way to the end of a bench, just as the lights dimmed. The curtain rose, and a pioneer man and woman burst predictably into a song about independence and a better life. Almost as soon as they'd begun singing, Buddy leaned against the wall of the theater and pulled me back to rest between his legs. "Buddy, stop it!" I whispered as he began nibbling my ear. "I'm trying to watch."

"First you're hot," he said. "Then you're cold."

"I'm not cold," I said. "Just not here!"

Buddy sat up and tried to listen, but I could see him in my peripheral vision fussing around in the dark. He traced the pattern on his boot with his finger, looked in his wallet, recombed his hair. All the while, his boot was tapping wildly against the ground. Finally, he slid off the bench and went outside while I bit my nails in the dark, watching the play to its excruciating finale.

I stood outside the theater afterward, thinking he'd return. Finally, I walked briskly out to the parking lot and found Buddy, palms against the hood of the Mercedes, while a Phoenix cop searched his pockets. For an absurd moment, I thought he'd lost his car keys, and that the cop was helping him find them. Buddy's face was turned, but I could see that his neck was bright red as the cop put the cuffs on him.

"This your boyfriend?" the cop asked me as I walked uncertainly to the car. I nodded.

"You look like a nice girl," he said, frowning, as he guided Buddy by the elbow to the backseat of the cruiser. "What are you doing running around with a boy who drives a hot car?"

"Hot?" I asked stupidly, thinking of weather.

"Stolen," the cop said, a decibel nicer, as if addressing the learning-impaired.

"I told you, I just drive them," said Buddy. He looked like a scared animal, sweaty and desperate. "I don't know where they're from."

"I followed you all the way from Phoenix," said the cop as he prodded Buddy into the car. "I don't know what you've done yet, mister," he said, "but I know you've done something." He slammed the door of the backseat and motioned for me to join him in the front.

The air conditioning in the cruiser wasn't working, so the fan merely moved the hot air around. I felt dizzy with fear and dehydration and the effort required to

My
Life
as a
girl

stare straight ahead. I was afraid to refer to my secret life stashed in the backseat, visible but mute behind the Plexiglas window. The cop offered me water from his canteen. "No, thank you," I croaked, my tongue turned to jerky in my mouth.

In Phoenix, the heat isn't weather—it's a live thing, visible in waves in the air. In the summer, it dries the sweat before it can collect on your forehead; it punches the hope right out of you first thing in the morning when you open the door. The heat, as I'd written in a letter to Amanda, is tolerable only if you've got central air and a swimming pool.

It wasn't until I viewed my life from the interior of a Phoenix police car that I began to understand for the first time how truly comfortable my life had been. Rosa told me stories of migrant farm workers collapsing in the lettuce fields, while waiting in the sun for buses, or crossing the border from Mexico in the middle of the night. People died all the time in Phoenix from heat, from what they call "exposure," while people like me carelessly lived their lives.

On the long drive back to Phoenix, I didn't have the energy or the faith to argue for my innocence, but the cop seemed to believe in it all the same. He asked me questions about college, not once alluding to the arrest record that would shoot down my plans.

Still, when he asked me for my address, I was sure he meant to pop in for a heart-to-heart with Mom. When we pulled up in front of our apartment, I waited for him to park the car and get out. Slowly, it dawned on me that he wasn't coming in, that there would be no consequences. I was astonished. He was just waiting politely for me to get out of his car.

"Go to college, have a nice life," the cop said sternly, as I stepped out onto the scalding asphalt. He jerked his neck toward the backseat, but I was too cowardly to look at Buddy. "And stay away from this bad boy."

"Yes, sir," I said. Then the cop drove off down our pretty palm-lined street to take my summer romance in for questioning.

Inside, I found Mom sitting on the couch in her day-off dress, drinking iced tea and watching the evening news. "Let's order out Mexican," she said. "It's too hot to cook."

"Sounds good to me," I said. Nothing, in fact, had ever sounded so good.

I sat down next to her and looked around the room, embracing the unfashionable furniture, beverage-stained carpet, glass-and-chrome stereo cabinet, sloping piles of books and magazines, every ordinary thing. We watched the rest of the news together in silence: house fire, drowning, seven heat-related deaths.

chapter

fifteen

By the time the plane landed in Phoenix, the business-
man sitting next to me had emptied four tiny bottles of
vodka and had all but proposed to the woman across
the aisle. My tooth still hurt, as if the right side of my
face were being blowtorched. I could turn the flame
down only by stretching my neck back and resting my
head against the seat. I stayed that way until the last
passenger had vacated, then I gathered my overhead
luggage and bump-dragged my way to the baggage
claim. There was my mother looking girlish in a pair of
blue jeans and an A.S.U. sweatshirt. She'd colored her
hair a gleaming auburn. She was smiling, waving.
Alone.

I put down my carry-on and limped to her, crying
already: for the pain in my jaw, but also because I
knew that, after the glow of reunion, we'd be bickering
about my father again. I cried because I was relieved
and terrified to find I was the same flawed person
who'd left Phoenix, just as Buddy had said. I cried
because I'd dreamed of a hero's homecoming, and
instead felt so small standing there sobbing and

embracing my mother next to the circling luggage
carousel. People passed us, rubbernecking as if
we were a traffic accident, their faces fixed with
knowing, sympathetic smiles.

Mom let me carry on for a few minutes, patting my back mechanically, the way you would
burp a baby. I felt her wedding band knock against my
shoulder blade. "Jaime," she said finally. "The verdict
is in."

I pulled away from her and felt my stolen Future
slip into its old place between us. "Why didn't you call
me?" I asked.

"I didn't want to upset you. You were taking
exams."

"So he's guilty," I said. "You think I didn't know
that?"

"Oh, Jaime," said Mom. Her hard smile stretched
across her face, making deep lines that would grow
deeper with years. This brave face masked her own
ambivalence—the love and hate she felt for my father
in the same breath sometimes—just as neatly as a scar
sealed a wound. "They found him innocent. Isn't it
wonderful? He'll be home on Christmas."

The traffic crawled on Central Avenue, the last leg of
my long trip home. Mom tuned to the news station to
find the source of the trouble. I stared glumly out the
window at the Christmas decorations along the avenue,
sombreroed Santas and plastic cacti draped with gaudy
beads. I knew I should be happy that Dad would be

coming home, but I felt a mix of longing and fear. I couldn't shake the feeling that history would soon repeat itself.

Mom turned off the radio. "Look," she said, pointing to a spot five miles distant. "See there? Smoke."

As we came nearer, we could see flames leaping from a gabled roof, curling black and oily against the sky. It was one of my favorites, a hundred-year-old farmhouse with two stories and an old-fashioned wrap-around porch. In high school, I used to pass the house every morning on the city bus, marveling that it had survived in a neighborhood of new construction, faux Spanish colonials built to mimic Rosa's.

"Oh, God," I said. "I loved that house."

Mom sighed. "What a shame."

"I can't look." But I stared, like everyone else, as we drove slowly past. In the front yard, firemen had planted a charred pole as a warning: the remains of a thirsty Christmas tree left too long alight.

"It happens every year," Mom said, shaking her head.

Finally we were home—or rather, at the Oasis. Our landlord had sandblasted the front wall of our apartment, but you could still make out Buddy's love note. It would probably still be there after we'd gone.

Inside, things were different, too, cleaner and more organized. The maple dresser was missing from Mom's bedroom, replaced with a prettier one stained antique

white. She'd bought a new floral bedspread and
had painted the walls a pale lavender, as if a new
color scheme would make my father behave.
Maybe, though, Mom had finally woken up and
would begin to take charge.

"What's up with your bedroom?" I asked, not
sure what I wanted to hear.

She shrugged and said simply, "It was time for
some changes."

"Good for you," I said, though I didn't like the
decor. I felt disoriented, the way I'd always felt in
Phoenix, where nothing was repaired, just demolished
and replaced with something new and bright and
promising. Before, I had looked to the East, to college,
to get my bearings. But now I just felt lost.

I told Mom I was going to Rosa's, but I found myself
heading north on Central instead of south. I told myself
I'd just drive by, check to make sure he was all right.
After I parked, I stopped telling myself anything, just
let my sneakered feet guide me across the brittle lawn
to the lighted window at the side of the house.

"You're lucky I didn't shoot you," Buddy said, a
startled expression on his face. He ducked under the
shade and opened his window. He was shirtless and
wore a pair of tattered Levis. It was unseasonably
warm for December. By Christmas the temperature
would rise to 85 degrees.

"Shoot me?" I said, laughing nervously. I felt light-
headed seeing him, like my brain had suffered a slow

leak. What had been alarming at Bryn Mawr was now reassuring: Buddy's skin, his scent, his mouth still defined my desire.

I touched his chest. He took my hand and placed it back on the sill. "Aren't you going to invite me in?" I asked.

"What for?"

"What for? Do I have to have a reason? I was on my way to Rosa's, and I wondered how you were."

Buddy's face softened then; he finally understood. "I've got some friends here," he warned me in a low voice. "But I could get rid of them."

"Do it then," I said. I wished he'd open the shade, so I could see past him to the party that had been going on in his room. I was sure Diane was there, with her hips whittled skinny from her body brace. Just behind my contempt was envy for girls like Diane, whose mothers weren't out to make sure that they were meant for better things. Girls who entered parties fearlessly, who went and picked the partners they wanted from the dance floor.

"Hold on," Buddy said, sliding the window closed. A few minutes later, he opened it again and helped me over the threshold.

"Don't move," he said, setting me down on the bed. "I'll be right back."

"Don't tell your mom I'm here," I whispered. "It'll be too weird." I didn't want to explain what I was doing there to anyone. Besides, Shelly would make me feel like a bug caught in a spider's web, as opposed to the concerned ex-girlfriend I wanted to believe I was. Buddy nodded and pulled the door shut behind him.

Somehow, I'd expected his room to be an archive of boyish affections: concert posters, dusty airplane models, the crushed lids of old game boxes peeking out from under the bed. Instead, it looked like a hand-me-down from a much older brother. The bed was queen-sized, spread with a cover made of some kind of fake bearish fur. Next to it stood a wooden night table like the one my parents had, littered with empty beer bottles and an overturned bottle of aspirin. In the corner, a bench and a barbell loaded with hundred-pound weights sat on a hairy, beige rug. Not a boy's room at all, but a monument to lost youth.

Curious, I pushed open a narrow door near the window and discovered that Buddy's bachelor pad included his own bathroom. Quickly, I checked my face in the mirror of the medicine cabinet, and then, as if it were an afterthought, opened it to reveal what was inside. Aftershave, a scummy razor, a comb, a cylinder of deodorant, a crusty tube of toothpaste. These everyday maintenance products caught me by surprise.

On the lower shelf was what I was seeking: Diane's abalone makeup mirror, frosted with cocaine dust. Finding it was like discovering an entire wing of rooms I never knew existed in a house I built myself. I ran my finger across the mirror and tasted the cocaine, welcoming the spreading numbness on the tip of my tongue.

My Life

as a

girl

"Jaime? What are you doing?" Buddy had caught me, mirror in hand.

"Your mom could find this stuff," I said.

Buddy took the mirror from me and put it back in the cabinet. "My mother doesn't come in here," he said. Then he flicked off the light and pulled me back to the bed.

Slowly, I moved my hand down his chest to his waistband, the way I'd practiced in my head. When I undid the brass button, Buddy sucked in his breath.

"Are you sure?" he asked, kneeling to tug at his zipper.

"I just want to touch you," I lisped, stumbling over my stupid tongue.

"I'll show you something better," Buddy whispered. He reached into the bedside drawer, tore the wrapper on a condom. When he kissed me, I pictured wheels spinning, neon lights flashing, poker chips being stacked up to the ceiling. Anything to hold on to the illusion that I was there to save him and not to lose myself.

chapter

sixteen

On Christmas Eve morning, Mom brought home a fake tree constructed like a hoop skirt, with ugly blue-green plastic branches bending every which way.

"It's fake," I said.

Mom snapped. "Would you rather have a fire?"

My bad tooth wailed in my ear like a siren. I held a scalding coffee mug against it, trying to distract myself with pain I could control. When Mom looked over at me, I was wincing and rubbing the hot spot the mug had left on my cheek.

"I think one of my molars is rotten," I blurted out.

"Let me see...For God's sake," she said when I clamped my mouth shut. "I'm your mother." She anchored her thumb under my chin and tugged at my lower lip with her index finger.

"Which one?" Mom asked, scrutinizing my teeth.

I tried to indicate with my tongue.

"I just can't tell," Mom said. She held my face in her hands, kneading the swollen spot under my jaw while she looked away expertly, frowning. My head resting in my mother's strong hands, I thought I could give up anything. Even Buddy.

"It hurts," I said, hoping Mom would hold me a little longer.

"Of course it does," Mom said. She took away her hands and prodded her own jaw gently, searching for similarities. "You should see Dr. Millstone right away."

"Can't we wait a little?" I whined. "See if it stops?"

"You've waited too long already," Mom decided. She rushed around the kitchen, rinsing out her coffee cup, flipping through her address book to find the dentist's number, dialing the phone. Mom was at her best in a crisis, more fully herself.

"What if, for instance, you were to bump someone who's coming in for a vanity procedure—say, dental bonding?" she suggested to the receptionist. "It's Christmas Eve, and my daughter is in pain." A minute later, she hung up the phone. "Full schedule, my butt," she said. "There are hidden openings in anyone's book."

"Bruxism, that's the problem," Dr. Millstone declared, prodding the culprit tooth. I lay back in the dentist's chair, staring up at his kind face. He had been treating me since I was a child. "It's not your fault," he said, poking among his instruments with his manicured fingers. "Your mother grinds her teeth, too."

Mom had told me about teeth grinding long ago, when she explained away other mysteries. The talk began with menstruation and moved on to bruxism, leading me to believe for a long time that the two conditions were related.

"There's not a virgin surface in her entire mouth," Dr. Millstone said, jerking his thumb toward the room where Mom waited, reading magazines. Then he went back to moving hammers and picks and files in and out of my numbed mouth, as though he had not said anything rude.

Dr. Millstone scraped the molar and filed it down to a clean stub. "When you grind away the filling," he explained, "there's nothing to keep the cavity from eating its way down to the roots." He didn't ask me why I ground my teeth. He wasn't interested in getting to the bottom of it. He went about fixing me with a bored, pleasant expression, reassuring me that what I suffered was fairly routine. "We'll fix it up so it doesn't show," Dr. Millstone promised. "We'll make you a brand-new tooth."

He left me reclining in the dentist's chair while he consulted with Mom behind the door. "The damage has been done," I heard him say, or thought I did. The codeine I'd been given seemed to enhance my aural powers. "The best thing to do is to cap it."

"Of course," I heard my mother say.

Driving home, Mom told me that Dr. Millstone would rush the job, replacing the temporary cap with a new, porcelain tooth the following week. "You're very lucky we caught it when we did," she said. "It was much worse for me." At a stoplight, she turned to me and pulled down her lower lip, exposing a molar. "See,

My
Life

as a

girl

you can hardly tell."

I looked at Mom sleepily. The tooth she revealed was perfectly white and even-edged, standing out oddly against her other, authentic teeth. "It's nice," I said, feeling generous from the drug, which had blocked the pain completely. "It doesn't look real."

Mom didn't want to leave me alone, blunted as I was by painkillers, but she had to go to work. "It doesn't hurt anymore," I said. To prove it, I slapped my swollen cheek.

"Your judgment is off just slightly," Mom said. "Please stay inside until I get home." She stood over a boiling pot on the stove, melting a small square of wax like the kind football players and my mother chewed on to keep from gnashing their teeth. When the wax was softened, she slipped it into my mouth. "Bite down," she said, and my teeth left an orderly impression in the cooled wax. "You should really wear the guard all day," Mom warned me.

As soon as she'd pulled out of the driveway, I removed the mouth guard. I went into her bathroom and dropped it into a glass of water with two of the effervescent tablets I'd seen her use. Then I placed the glass next to hers on the vanity and watched the bubbles rise.

While replacing the tablets in the cabinet beneath the sink, I found a bag of licorice, which Mom loved, but which Dr. Millstone had forbidden. It made me feel

desperate to think of my mother hiding in the
bathroom chewing candy, her teeth mired in
black sweetness, grinding away. I threw the
licorice to the back of the cabinet and covered it
up with a bag of cotton balls.

I knew Mom didn't like me going through her
things, but I felt somehow entitled after what I'd suffered that morning. Besides, finding the candy was
like permission. I began opening and shutting cabinets, looking inside without knowing what I was looking for.

I slid open one of the vanity drawers and there,
with the dusty cases of eye shadow my mother kept but
never wore, was a lipstick. Its gold-plated case was
rubbed to dull gray in places, and the deep red color
was worn to a waxy stub. I recognized the color from
photos of Mom's high school days, before she'd met
Dad and switched to frosted pink.

I picked up the lipstick and drew exaggerated lips
over my own. I studied myself in the mirror, pleased
and repulsed by what I saw.

When I heard Buddy pull up in his Mustang, I
wiped my mouth with a tissue, put the tube in my jeans
pocket, and went out to meet him.

chapter

seventeen

"Be careful with me," I yelled over the stereo as I got into Buddy's car. "I'm high on codeine."

"Cool," Buddy said, and fishtailed out of the driveway. He turned the stereo up louder and pumped the brakes at every stoplight, making the car lurch on the downbeat of a Rolling Stones song. I felt myself being shaken, emptied out as easily as if my skin were tissue, and filled up again with music. I heard the song even after it was over and Buddy turned off the stereo.

"Jaime?" he said.

"Present," I answered.

Buddy gripped the steering wheel and stared straight ahead. "What's the drug for?" he asked. "Some girl thing?"

"Yes," I said. I tried to sound reasonable, though I felt as if I were standing outside myself, telling myself. Several minutes later, I added, "Don't worry, you can't catch it."

"Catch what?" Buddy said, newly concerned.

"Forget it."

I was relieved when we turned onto the highway. I

looked out the passenger window, grateful for the
metal barrier of the door, which separated me
from the desert outside. I watched mile markers,
cacti, and telephone poles speed past us, blur-
ring together. Under the harsh noon sun, the
landscape appeared flat and endless.

Soon I felt myself slipping out the window, following my own gaze. I shut my eyes immediately to stop it,
and prodded the cap with my tongue, trying to recall
what the ache had felt like. But already it was like
something that had happened to someone else a long
time ago.

I opened my eyes again as Buddy suddenly veered
off the highway and into the desert. Low brush slapped
at the Mustang, and rocks shot off the tires. A cloud of
dust followed the car, hovering around us when we
finally stopped.

"Here we are," he said. The car stood in idle,
shaking and humming with air conditioning. Without
warning, he turned to me and reached under my T-
shirt.

"Wait," I gasped, feeling a half-beat behind. "I'm
still sort of buzzed."

"That must be good stuff," he said, kissing my
neck.

I pushed him away. "I don't like it," I said, and
heard my own voice echo.

"I know what you like," Buddy whispered. I heard
it over and over again in my head.

I let him place me beneath him, so that I lay

My
Life

as a

girl

uncomfortably across the bucket seats. I craned my neck and tried to kiss him, but my lips felt inflated and I was distracted by the roar of the air conditioner. Maybe I could just lie here, I thought, and he would keep petting my hair the way he was doing. The repetitive motion helped me tell who was who.

He reached under my shirt again.

"The atmosphere's all wrong," I complained.

"Close your eyes then," said Buddy, but that only made it worse. I could feel him struggle out of his clothes and fling them into the backseat. His urgency seemed unnecessary to me and a bit ridiculous. I began to giggle as he yanked off my shoes and socks.

"What are you laughing at?" he asked.

"It tickles," I lied. I was startled by the car door opening, my bare feet reaching out to meet warm air.

"Legroom," Buddy said, out of breath.

"Can anyone see?" I asked, opening my eyes.

Buddy kneeled over me, naked and sweating, trying to find a place to put his knees. He didn't look like himself; his body was larger, and his eyes bulged obscenely from the heat. I began to laugh again, covering my mouth like a guilty child.

Buddy ignored me, adjusting the air vents to blast at our bodies. Behind him, in the distance, cars passed on the highway.

"Next time, wear a skirt," he grumbled, unbuttoning my jeans and tugging them down to my knees. The lipstick, which had worked its way out of my front pocket, fell onto the floor. I reached for it, trying to conceal it in my palm.

"What's that?" Buddy said, uncurling my fingers. "You never wear lipstick."

"I do now," I said.

"Let's see." He popped open the case with his thumb. "Smokin' color," he said. He held my jaw steady and carefully traced my lips, biting his own as he concentrated, which confused me. *Why doesn't it hurt?* I wondered, watching his mouth.

After he'd finished, he sat back on his heels and frowned at me, as though he disapproved. "Go like this," he said, rubbing his lips together as he'd seen Diane do. "So it'll stick."

I tried, but my lips bulged like balloons. I couldn't get a grip on them.

"Come on—look sexy," he said. I scowled and stuck out my tongue, the way the Wynn sisters always did in family photos. "That's real pretty, Jaime," he said.

I couldn't believe the way I was acting, but I felt somehow I had to go along with it. At some point during the drive, I had stepped out of my body, and I knew it was just a matter of time before I'd be able to enter it again. I was trying to be patient. Though I was grateful for the codeine cap on my pain, I didn't like the way the drug made everything ordinary seem strange. If I hadn't known Buddy better, I would have thought he was dangerous.

I looked around desperately for something familiar,

and was relieved to find his Stetson hanging crookedly from the rearview mirror. "Put your hat on," I whispered.

"Anything to get you in the mood," he said, grabbing the hat and setting it far back on his head. "Well?" the hat said, while Buddy moved his lips.

To avoid answering, I grabbed the hat with both hands and pulled Buddy down on top of me. As I kissed him, feigning passion, I began to really feel it.

"Diane," he whispered.

"Shhh," I said.

From a distance, I watched myself slide my hands across his oily back, across his air-cooled hips. I forgot to concentrate on staying in place, though, and so I found myself drifting out of the car and across the shimmering desert toward home. There, Rosa and the Wynn sisters waited at a table cluttered with empty beer bottles and plates streaked with tomato sauce.

"Did you hear that?" I asked Mom, pointing at the bodies that wrangled with each other in the car. "Did you hear him say 'Diane'?"

"It's a shame," said Mom.

"It just goes to show you," said Jo Ellen.

"Thank the Lord our mother told us we were meant for better things," added Henri.

"Dump him," said Rosa. "It's about time."

"You're so hot," Buddy said to the girl who lay beneath him in the front seat of the car. He sounded slightly nervous, but appreciative.

Crashing against Buddy, my body was
returned to me. I felt his real, crushing weight,
the way his ribs rocked, then settled against
mine. Trapped beneath him on the slippery plastic seats, I felt like crying. Almost as a reflex, I
held on to him tighter.

"Hey!" Buddy said, as my hand, reattached to my
intentions, knocked the Stetson off his head. The hat
blew across the bucket seats, caught by a gust from the
air conditioner, and tumbled onto the ground. Buddy
lifted his head and looked between me and his lost
possession for a moment. Then he eased himself off me
and leaped naked from the car to chase it.

I sat up and watched as the hat flew in circles in
the air, suspended momentarily by a dust devil. Buddy
jumped and reached foolishly for it, his limbs flailing
and genitals bouncing. I felt myself jump with him,
though in reality I remained in the car, calmly pulling
on my T-shirt and wriggling back into my jeans. I was
dressed by the time Buddy pinned the hat to the
ground. I scooted over into the driver's seat.

He turned and waved the dirty hat at me like a
rodeo cowboy, shouting my name, his body streaked
with muddy sweat. I waved back and honked the horn
at him.

Buddy was still hollering and waving as I closed
the car door and shifted into drive. When I stepped on
the gas and spun the tires in the dirt, he began to run
after me.

I drove toward the highway, watching Buddy follow

My

Life

as a

girl

in the rearview mirror. Eventually, he stopped chasing me. He held the hat against his groin and hopped in place to keep the bare soles of his feet from burning. Finally, deferring to pain over pride, he dropped the hat on the ground and stood on it.

I kept driving until he was the right size to suit me, a distant speck contained in the two-by-eight rectangle of the mirror. I looked ahead, up the burned black gloss of highway leading back to Phoenix. I looked back and saw Buddy dancing on a hat in the dirt, a boy as helpless as I sometimes felt. Somebody's father someday. Somebody's son. I knew I could leave him out there, forever a villain, the way my mother had Spider Reid. Instead, I turned the car around to retrieve him and drove straight back into the dust cloud I'd made.

I couldn't look at Buddy as I pulled up beside him.

He made a false move toward the driver's seat, then hopped to the passenger side with his hat between his ankles. "A guy could die out there," he said. His cracking voice, the slump of his shoulders, told me that he knew I'd bet against him. He dressed quickly, his back turned, trying to hide his body from me.

I didn't have my own words then for the sadness I felt. I thought of what Rosa's mom had said, that giving yourself away was like giving away pearls. I thought I understood this that day in the desert, though I wouldn't really understand it until I met the man

I would marry and mourned what I'd squandered: my body, my privacy, my trust.

Instead I accused him. "You slept with Diane."

For once, Buddy didn't lie to me. He said over his shoulder, "Because you were never coming back."

We were even, then. My faithlessness was every bit as wretched as his.

But then a weird thing happened: Buddy laughed. It wasn't haughty laughter, but helpless. His laughter was contagious, escaping the shaking car and spreading itself across the barren landscape. Pretty soon I was laughing, too.

"You really had me going there," he said, and smiled.

EPILOGUE

The disappearance of my money was a topic left so long in storage that by the time I unpacked it—years later, after college, when I was working to support myself in medical school—I had almost forgotten about it. Then one day I received a check for $5,000, which I deposited in the Philadelphia bank account I'd opened in my own name. With it was a note—For school, love, Dad. There was no mention of the old debt to my Future that was finally being repaid.

The check seemed, for one grace-filled moment when I opened the envelope, like a gift. Years do that: they grind away at anger's sharp edges until one day you find that what you hold in your heart isn't anger at all, but something as blunt and elegant as understanding, or even forgiveness.

ABOUT THE AUTHOR

ELIZABETH MOSIER was raised in Arizona, the setting for *My Life as a Girl* and for her short stories, which have appeared in *Sassy*, *Seventeen*, *The Philadelphia Inquirer Magazine*, and various literary magazines. A graduate of Bryn Mawr College, she lives outside Philadelphia with her husband and two children, and directs Bryn Mawr's summer writing program for high school students. This is her first novel.